# THE MAN FROM U.N.C.L.E.

**THE STONE-COLD DEAD IN THE MARKET AFFAIR**

**U.N.C.L.E.**

# THE MAN FROM U.N.C.L.E.

## THE STONE-COLD DEAD IN THE MARKET AFFAIR

## JOHN ORAM

Based on the cult TV spy series

B⬢XTREE

Published in the UK 1993 by
BOXTREE LIMITED
Broadwall House
21 Broadwall
London SE1 9PL

First published in the UK 1965 by Souvenir Press in association with The New English Library.

First published in the USA 1965 by Ace Books Inc.

10 9 8 7 6 5 4 3 2 1

© 1964–1968 Turner Entertainment Co.
All rights reserved.
Licensed by Copyright Promotions Ltd.

No part of this publication may be reproduced or transmitted, in any form or by any means, without permission of the publishers.

Cover photograph courtesy of The Kobal Collection.
Cover design by Head Design.

Typesetting by DP Photosetting, Aylesbury, Bucks.
Printed and bound by Cox & Wyman Ltd, Reading, Berkshire.

ISBN: 1 85283 857 4

Except in the United States of America, this book is sold subject to the condition that it shall not, by way of trade or otherwise, be lent, resold, hired out or otherwise circulated without the publisher's prior consent in any form of binding or cover other than that in which it is published and without a similar condition including this condition being imposed on a subsequent purchaser.

A catalogue record for this book is available from the British Library.

# PROLOGUE

FROM BLODWEN　　　　　　TO W
　NEWPORT MON　　　　　　SECTION 1 (P)
　　SOUTH WALES　　　　　UNCLE NEW YORK
　SECRETEST: STREET FATALITY HERE TODAY PRODUCED BUMPER BUNDLE MINTWISE STOP SUSPECT BROWN BIRD SINGING STOP SUGGEST RELATIVES ATTEND URGENTEST STOP

TO BLODWEN　　　　　　　FROM W
　NEWPORT MON　　　　　　SECTION 1 (P)
　　SOUTH WALES　　　　　UNCLE NEW YORK
　SECRETEST: DESPATCH SPECIMEN BEQUEST IMMEDIATE STOP RUSSIAN COUSIN TRANSITING STOP TRY LOCATE NEST STOP

FROM BLODWEN　　　　　　TO W
　NEWPORT MON　　　　　　SECTION 1 (P)
　　SOUTH WALES　　　　　UNCLE NEW YORK
　SECRETEST: WILCO BUT NAME BLODWEN NOT CASSANDRA STOP CASE OF NEEDLE HAYSTACKWISE STOP AND NO THREADS STOP.

# CHAPTER ONE

MARKET STREET in Newport, Monmouthshire, bears no resemblance to its namesake in San Francisco. It is around three hundred yards long, narrow, shabby, with an atmosphere redolent of gasoline, printer's ink, fish, vegetables and good Welsh beer.

It is bounded on one side by the grey stone outer wall of the old municipal covered market, and on the other by a conglomeration of premises which include a branch of a multiple tailoring firm, the van bay and editorial entrance of the *South Wales Argus*, wholesale fruit, vegetable and fish merchants, and a store specializing in workmen's clothing.

There are two taverns in the street's three-hundred-yard length. The man in the shabby fawn trench-coat visited each in turn.

He was a small, slim man of about thirty years of age. His face was pasty, with high cheekbones accentuated by the sunken flesh below. His hair was a thin thatch that looked like bleached hay. His curiously pale green eyes, set close to a button nose, held an expression of abject fright.

He went into the cream-washed bar of the Black Swan and bought a glass of beer and a sandwich. The chicken sandwiches at the Black Swan are worth travelling a long way to sample, but the man in the trench-coat gulped his down as if it were tasteless. His little green eyes roved over the back of the bar, resting briefly on the miner's lamp on the top shelf and the ship's bell over the door to the landlord's private quarters. Then he drank his beer quickly and left without a word.

He hurried along the street and pushed open the door of the saloon bar of the Cross Keys. Except for a pretty girl sitting alone by the counter, the big room was empty. Again the man's eyes searched the bottle-filled shelves. Perched perkily between two thirds of Long John whisky there was a little doll in Welsh national costume. Some of the tension went out of the man's face. He rapped on the counter for service.

The barmaid came from the back bar, where a juke box was playing an Andy Williams number. A big, handsome, black-haired woman in a black, close-fitting dress, she could have stepped straight out of a Manet painting. She smiled and said good morning as if she really meant it.

The man said: 'A pint of bitter.' Then, nodding towards the doll: 'You don't get many of those around here, I suppose?'

'No. A friend of the missis brought it from Cardiff for a present. Pretty, isn't it?'

'Yes.' The man seemed satisfied. He took the beer and went to sit at the far end of the room. He was careful to choose a seat from which he could watch both the door and the big window that looked out on to the street. After a token sip he did not touch the beer on the table in front of him.

The girl at the counter said quietly: 'A sociable type.'

'You get all kinds,' the barmaid said. 'I never saw him in here before.'

'Ah, well!' She pushed her empty glass across the counter. 'Fill it up again.'

Mixing the gin and vermouth the barmaid asked: 'You staying long in Newport, love?' Her husky voice with its attractive Welsh lilt contrasted strongly with the girl's clipped London accent.

'A few days, maybe. It depends.'

'Just on holiday, like?'

'You could call it that.' The girl lifted her glass. 'Cheers! You sure you won't have one?'

'No, thank you, love. Too early for me.'

The bar door opened and two men walked in. Both were six-footers, dressed in discreet business suits. One wore a navy-blue raincoat.

Their effect on the man in the trench-coat was electrical. He jumped to his feet, overturning the table, and charged between them, his eyes wild and staring.

As the door swung behind him, one of the men asked, astonished: 'What the hell was that all about?'

'Must of thought you were coppers,' the barmaid said.

There came an agonized screech of brakes from the street outside. Women screamed. There was a confused babel of voices.

'My God! an accident.' The barmaid whipped up the counter flap and ran across the room with the girl beside her. The two big men were already on the sidewalk.

A lorry loaded with heavy crates was blocking the narrow street. Under its front wheels was all that remained of the man in the shabby trench-coat. The driver, a grey-faced kid in patched blue overalls, was vomiting uncontrollably against the lorry's bonnet. His mate, dazed but articulate, was protesting: 'We 'adn't got no chance. 'E dashed right out of the pub straight under our wheels.'

But few of the crowd were listening. They were too busy picking up the hundreds of brand-new currency notes which littered the street.

A boy in a white coat was incredulously counting a handful of fivers. The girl put her hand on his arm. 'Where did all the money come from?'

'Gawd knows,' he said. 'Out of 'is pockets, I suppose. 'E must've been a walking Bank of England. You seen a copper, miss? I got to 'and this over quick or I'll be tempted.'

The girl waited until the police, ambulance and breakdown appliances had arrived. She watched the broken

11

body taken from beneath the wheels and put on to a stretcher. Then she made her way up Market Street and across the High Street to the General Post Office.

She went into a public telephone booth and dialled a number.

'From Blodwen, Newport, Mon, South Wales,' she dictated, 'To W., Section I (P)...'

# CHAPTER TWO

WHEN THE telephone bell cut harshly into the Shostakovitch symphony, Illya Kuryakin was less than delighted. He had just showered and shaved after a profitless twelve-hour stake-out of a house in the crummier section of the Bronx, and he had been looking forward to a lazy morning in the small, untidy apartment he called home.

He switched off the heat under the coffee percolator, muted the volume of the record player and picked up the receiver. 'Kuryakin.'

The girl at the other end of the wire said brightly: 'Good morning. I hope I didn't disturb anything.'

'Only my dreams. In another ten minutes I should have been in bed.'

'Too bad,' she sympathized. 'No beddy-byes for you, I'm afraid. The big white chief is waiting.'

'That man!' he said bitterly. 'He knows I've been up all night.'

'So sue him,' she advised. 'In ten minutes, then?'

'I'll be there.'

He replaced the receiver, set the coffee pot boiling again, and began to dress.

Exactly ten minutes later he paid off his cab in front of Del Floria's tailoring ship in the middle of a brownstone block near the United Nations headquarters. He ran down the three steps into the shop, took off his jacket and handed it to the little grey-haired Italian. He said: 'The usual.'

Del nodded and pushed the button by the side of his pressing machine. Illya walked into the third 'try-on' cubicle at the back of the shop, drew the curtain and turned a clothes-hook on the rear wall. The wall swung away silently and he walked through to the Admissions desk.

The girl on the desk had watched his entry on her closed-circuit TV screen and was ready with the white badge which would admit him to the third floor – the domain of U.N.C.L.E.'s Policy and Operations department. She pinned the badge to his lapel almost caressingly. The sober-faced little Russian had that effect upon most women.

Illya stepped into the elevator and rode up to the third floor. He went to the armoury, drew his favourite P38 automatic pistol, checked the mechanism and tucked it into the shoulder holster under his left arm. Then he walked along the corridor to Mr Alexander Waverly's private office.

There were two men in the room. Mr Waverly, the lean, dry chief of Section 1 (Policy and Operations) was standing by the big window which looked out on to the East River and the United Nations building. Napoleon Solo, chief enforcement agent for U.N.C.L.E. sat at the huge O-shaped table which dominated the room. Before him were stacked neat piles of currency – kroner, Reichmarks, dollars and pounds.

Illya said: 'Good morning. Going into Wall Street?'

Mr Waverly turned. 'Ah! Mr Kuryakin. Thank you for coming so promptly. You will be flying to Britain in an hour. So sit down, please, and read these.'

Illya took the three flimsies and scanned them, lingering over the third.

'Blodwen appears to have a sense of humour,' he said.

'I am glad you think so,' Mr Waverly said coldly.

'"Brown bird singing",' Illya read aloud. 'That's obviously our old friend Thrush. But "bumper bundle mintwise"?'

Mr Waverly gestured towards the stacks of notes on the O-shaped table. 'Those are specimens. What do you make of them?'

Illya picked up a 500-kroner note, an American ten-dollar bill and an English five-pound note. He took them across to the window and examined them carefully. 'They look all right to me,' he said at last.

'You would be prepared to spend them?'

His eyes lit hopefully. 'Can I?'

'If you did, you would end inevitably in gaol,' Mr Waverly said. 'They are all forgeries.'

'But they're perfect!'

'Almost perfect,' Napoleon Solo corrected. 'In every case the paper is slightly wrong. Take the Bank of England notes: they look right and they feel right – but the metal thread running through the paper is fractionally too thick. There's a similar infinitesimal flaw in all the others. But the printing is fantastically good. The forgers have either got access to the original plates – which on the face of it is impossible – or else they've succeeded in making exact copies.'

'That's been done before,' Illya said. 'Some kind of photographic process.'

Mr Waverly shook his head. 'No. With a photographic reproduction, the same number appears on every note. On these, you will observe, the numbers are random.'

'Then how is it done?'

'That,' said Mr Waverly, 'is what you are flying to Britain to find out. We know neither how nor where the notes are made. But we must find the answer quickly. You are intelligent enough to realize the disaster which would follow if Thrush were allowed to flood the world's markets with these almost indetectable forgeries. There would be financial panic. The economy of every country would collapse like the proverbial house of cards.'

Illya nodded. 'I see that. But what's the background? Blodwen's "street fatality" doesn't tell me much.'

Mr Waverly sat down at the table, took a brier pipe from the pocket of his shabby tweed jacket and began to turn it between his hands. He said: 'I can give you only the facts as Blodwen has reported them. An unidentified man arrives in the important Welsh seaport of Newport, Monmouthshire, and visits two inns in Market Street. For all we know, he may already have visited other establishments in the town. He is obviously a stranger to the district. He speaks with an uneducated English accent, nothing like the local intonation, and he has to find a Welsh doll to know that he has come to the right place.'

'Couldn't he have been told the name of the inn,' Solo objected. 'Wouldn't that be above the door?'

'It was painted along the entire length of the front wall above the window,' Mr Waverly said. 'That might argue, of course, that our man was an illiterate.'

'Or the doll could have been a signal?'

'No. We checked that. The doll had stood on the shelf for many months. But let me continue –

'The man orders a pint of beer, which he does not drink. He sits at a table, plainly waiting for someone. Two men come through the door. Our man panics. He dashes out into the street, straight under the wheels of a truck, Immediately, bank notes worth a small fortune are scattered all over the roadway. When his body is taken to the morgue, more bundles of notes are found stitched inside his trench-coat and suit linings. As nearly as we can estimate he was carrying on his person assorted forged currency to the face value of one hundred thousand dollars.'

Illya whistled soundlessly. He said: 'And no clue to where he came from?'

'None. His description was circulated to police stations, published in the evening newspapers and broadcast over radio and television. Nobody has come forward to identify him. Inquiries are proceeding, but you must remember that Newport is a town of more than 105,000 inhabitants, with a large floating population of seamen – to say nothing of the people who come in and out from the mining valleys and from the Welsh capital, Cardiff, only a few miles away.'

Solo asked: 'What about the two men who frightened him?'

Mr Waverly said: 'We have checked them. They were tunnellers working on one of the big Monmouthshire motorway projects. They were on holiday in Newport and just happened to call at the inn for a drink. Probably, as the barmaid suggested, our man took them for detectives.'

Illya picked up the third flimsy. '"Needle haystack-wise",' he quoted. 'Lady, you ain't kidding.'

Mr Waverly put the unlit pipe back in his pocket and stood up with an air of finality.

'You have not much time to catch your plane, Mr Kuryakin,' he said. 'You will fly direct to Rhoose, the Cardiff airport, and a car will take you on to Newport. Contact Blodwen as soon as you arrive. Is there anything else you wish to know?'

'Just one thing,' Illya said gloomily. 'Where do I pick up my crystal ball?'

# CHAPTER THREE

THE GIRL sitting on a stool at the bar counter was in her late twenties. Her close-cut, shining black hair framed an oval face of almost gipsy swarthiness. Her big eyes were deep hazel, fringed with long curling lashes. The hands that cradled a glass of gin and vermouth were brown and well-shaped, with slender, sensitive fingers. She wore a fluffy white nylon coat over a black cashmere sweater and tight white sharkskin pants. Her shoes, narrow-pointed, high-topped, like those of a mediaeval page-boy, were in scarlet suede. A tiny grey poodle, no bigger than a kitten, was sleeping placidly in her lap. She looked as out of place in a Welsh seaport pub as a rabbi at a christening.

She looked up when Illya came in, eyed him disinterestedly, then returned to her desultory conversation with an elderly man who looked like a travelling salesman.

The barmaid appeared, smiling, from the public bar, where the jukebox was blaring lustily. Illya ordered a Scotch on the rocks, and she said: 'I don't often get asked for that. Are you an American?'

'Does it show?'

'Not too much, love. I shouldn't worry about it.' She laughed throatily.

The salesman had gone and the girl was sitting alone. Illya gestured with his glass towards the poodle and asked: 'Did it take you long to knit that?'

She said, unoffended: 'Don't bother, chum. We've heard them all.' She scratched the dog's head. It blinked black shoebutton eyes and yawned widely, showing teeth like tiny ivory needles.

Illya said: 'Will you join me? I hate drinking alone.'

'If you twist my arm.' She slid the glass to the barmaid. 'Same again, dear.' Then to Illya: 'Slightly off your course, aren't you, sailor?'

'Not really. I'm travelling for my uncle.'

'Yes,' she said. 'I thought you might be.' She raised her refilled glass. 'Here's to him, bless his cotton socks.'

They finished their drinks in companionable silence, and then the girl got down from her stool.

'Sorry,' she said, 'but I must leave you. Got to take the pooch for an airing.' She smiled at the barmaid. 'Same old routine every day. Twice around Belle Vue Park, and then home for tea.'

'It's nice up by there,' the barmaid agreed, 'especially now, with all the dahlias out. See you to-morrow?'

'Maybe.' The girl attached a thin scarlet lead to the poodle's jewelled collar. The little dog pattered out beside her, looking like a bug on a string.

Illya bought another whisky and drank it slowly. Then he walked out into Market Street, made his way to the Dock Street terminus and after some inquiries boarded a bus for Stow Hill.

The conductor put him off at Stow Park Avenue and he walked down the hill, past tall houses that seemed to be occupied almost entirely by doctors and surgeons, to the wrought-iron gates of Belle Vue Park.

The girl was sitting on a yellow bench by a ring of trees that enclosed a druid's circle. Beyond the trees grassland swept down to the Cardiff road and the ultramarine-painted buildings of the giant Whitehead steelworks. Behind was the vast panorama of the docks, with the Bristol Channel a shining silver ribbon on the far horizon.

'Nice spot,' Illya said.

'Peaceful,' the girl agreed. 'At least, it is now. I'm not sure about the past.' She pointed to the ring of rough-hewn stones. 'That flat one in the middle was the sacrificial altar. You can see the little step where the Imperial Wizard, or whatever they called him, got to work with the cleaver. I suppose the other boys stood around and cheered.'

'Cosy!'

'Yes. I can never figure out whether it's a genuine relic or just something dumped down to amuse the kids ... So you're my Russian cousin?'

He made a formal bow. 'Illya Kuryakin. And you are Blodwen – or should I say Cassandra?'

She grinned. 'I thought that would get under the old buzzard's skin. Not that it isn't true. This business is a stinker. That's why I yelled for help.'

'I'm glad you did,' he said, with a warmth which would have annoyed the girl on U.N.C.L.E.'s Admissions desk. 'Have there been any developments?'

'A few. The police have identified the departed. He was a small-time crook from the Birmingham area. Nothing on his sheet but petty larcenies. God knows how he got involved in this set-up. It seems he came into Newport by long-distance bus from Corwen, a little market town in Merionethshire, North Wales. What he had been doing there is anybody's guess. He had been released from Walton Prison, Liverpool, about a month ago.'

She put the poodle on the ground and stood up. 'Let's walk a little. The park is worth seeing. For my money, it's one of the most beautiful in Britain.'

Released from its lead, the poodle bounced over the grass, yapping joyously in a high-pitched key, its big ears flapping like wings.

'One of these days,' Blodwen said, as they followed, 'she's going to take off and fly. The first jet-propelled pooch in history.'

Illya said: 'So he could have picked up the money either in Liverpool or somewhere in North Wales. The question is where he was taking it.'

She shrugged. 'Obviously, he was just a courier. My

bet is that whoever met him in the pub would have taken the cash down to the docks. There's a big trade between Newport, Russia and the Scandinavian ports, and it would be no trick to smuggle the stuff aboard a ship. I think the idea was to start distribution in Europe, not in Britain. That would be logical.'

'Have none of the notes shown up here?'

'A few. One or two fivers in Newport and a couple in Cardiff. But the police traced them back to the big scramble in Market Street. They didn't come from the main stream – wherever that is.'

They strolled past the children's playground, where West Indians, Arabs, Sikhs, Chinese and whites from the mean streets of dockland crowded the swings and chutes in noisy amity. The bright print frocks of the little girls made the place look like an animated flower garden.

They stopped to watch, and Illya said: 'Integration at last. It seems a pity they have to grow up.'

'Oh, I don't know. There's no colour problem in Newport or Cardiff. The races have been living together for years. They've learned to get along with each other.' She smiled suddenly. 'Maybe it's because we're a minority nation ourselves.'

He said, surprised: 'But you're not Welsh?'

'Back to the sixteenth century, both sides of the family,' she said. 'Don't let the voice fool you. My grandmother was one of the last of the great Welsh witches.'

'That figures,' he admitted. 'The spell lingers.'

They walked on towards the red-brick bulk of the Royal Gwent Hospital which overshadows the eastern end of the park.

Illya said quietly: 'Don't look now, dearie, but we're being followed.'

'You're joking, of course.'

'No. He's a medium-sized character with grey hair and a cavalry moustache, and he's wearing a sheepskin jacket. I noticed him dodging around the mulberry bush as I came into the park. And he's still tailing.'

She laughed. 'It's your suspicious nature. He's probably just an innocent bystander.'

'I don't think so. But we can soon find out. Let's get off the main path.'

'All right, Sherlock.' She turned to the right and headed across the grass towards a circle of eight weather-gnarled may trees.

'You know,' she said, 'this park is a kind of living history book. These trees were planted to commemorate the last-ditch stand of the First Monmouthshire Regiment between Wieltze and Verlorenhoek in 1915. Somewhere around a thousand men went into the line. Only a handful came out alive. But they did what they had to do. They stopped the German advance. Now, every spring, these trees are a cloud of blossom. I guess you couldn't find a lovelier memorial anywhere.'

'That's how people are around here. When something big happens, they plant trees. Over there –' she pointed to the left '– another ring marks the arrival of the first U.S. naval contingent in World War II.' Her voice changed. 'And you're dead right, brother. We've got company.'

The man in the sheepskin coat was bending down, ostentatiously studying the metal plaque that told of the coming of the American forces.

Beyond the may trees Illya saw a terrace thickly bordered by trees and bushes. He said: 'Make for the steps. Move fast. When you get to the top, duck into the shrubbery.'

Blodwen picked up the poodle and ran, with Illya close on her heels.

The shadower was taken by surprise. He straightened, and after a momentary hesitation pounded up the steps in pursuit. As he reached the top Illya stepped from behind the bushes and chopped down with an expert karate blow. The man crumpled. His head hit the paving with a hollow sound, and he lay still.

Illya said: 'Now, my friend, we'll see who you are.'

He yanked open the sheepskin jacket and searched swiftly. The inside breast pocket of the man's hairy tweed sports coat yielded a leather wallet and two envelopes. The wallet contained a driving licence in the name of John Carney, a few receipted bills and ten one-pound notes. The envelopes bore the inscription: 'John Carney, Esq, The Paddocks, Llandrillo, Merioneth.' One contained a final demand for water rates; the other, a bookmaker's account.

Illya memorized the name and address, then replaced the wallet and envelopes where he had found them. He put his hands under the man's armpits and dragged him to a bench. Then, with an effort, he hoisted him into a sitting position.

Blodwen, cuddling the poodle, emerged from the shelter of the trees. 'Is he...?' She let the sentence tail off apprehensively.

'Certainly not,' Illya said indignantly. 'I detest violence. He'll have a headache when he wakes, but that won't be for an hour or so. Meanwhile, I suggest we get out of here.'

They made their way to the gates leading into Friars Road, climbed the hill and emerged by St Woollo's Cathedral. Illya pointed to the bus stop. 'Back to town?'

'No. We'd better go to my place. I have a feeling we'll be safer under cover for a while.'

Blodwen's apartment was on the top floor of a stone-built Victorian house overlooking the Civic Centre. The windows gave a view of distant green mountains marred by sprawling new suburbs. The living-room furniture was a comfortable mixture of good pieces and auction-mart bargains. There was a big radiogram in a teak cabinet and a television set with a 23-inch screen. The wall-to-wall grey carpet gave evidence that the poodle had been hard to train.

Blodwen took off her coat and flung it on to a Danish-type settee upholstered in royal blue fabric. In the tight black sweater and narrow-hipped pants she looked like a ballet dancer. Only, Illya amended with satisfaction, better stacked. She put a Mancini long-player on the turntable, flicked the switch, and opened a wall-cupboard. 'Scotch, gin, vodka or rye?'

Illya settled himself in an elderly, chintz-covered armchair. 'Scotch will be find.'

She went into the pint-size kitchen and returned with a bowl of ice cubes from the refrigerator. As she poured the drinks she asked: 'So what did you learn about our woolly chum?'

'I got his name and address. Wait. I'll have to write them down. The place reads like a new kind of instant cake mix.'

He picked up a newspaper, scribbled in the margin and passed it to her.

She read aloud: 'Llandrillo, Merioneth ...That's interesting. Corwen's in Merioneth, too. It can't be coincidence.'

She took an A.A. guide from a row of books on the chimneypiece and thumbed the pages. 'Here we are. Merioneth. Corwen is on the branch railway line from Ruabon to Barmouth. '(That'll be closed down now, of course. Dear old Doctor Beeching, though you wouldn't know about him.) And – well, well! Would you believe it? – Llandrillo just happens to be the next village along the line – only five miles away.'

Illya took a thoughtful pull at his drink. 'I think,' he said slowly. 'I had better take a look at your North Welsh countryside. It gets more interesting by the minute.'

'Want me to come, too?'

He sighed. 'You'll never know how much,' he said. 'But just for the moment you had better stay here and hold the fort. Meanwhile, I think we'll call for reinforcements.'

'The legendary Mr Solo?'

'Who else?'

She crossed the room and turned the volume control at the side of the television set. The screen swung away, revealing a black, military-type radio transmitter.

'Be my guest,' she said.

# CHAPTER FOUR

THE BATTERED Ford Zephyr trundled leisurely along through little villages with unpronounceable Welsh names and it was uphill all the way. There were frequent stops while Illya confirmed his map bearings and not a few unscheduled halts to let the engine get its breath back for another climb.

The car nosed into Corwen around five in the afternoon. Near the market place Illya found a large ironmongery store bearing the improbable name of Jones. A friendly assistant inside directed him to the Cader Idris as being an hotel where they spoke English and took foreigners from across the border.

It was a comfortable, old-fashioned tavern with a great deal of old oak, gleaming brass and a permanent smell of boiled cabbage. And it was tactically situated in the High Street between a chapel hall and a cinema (Saturdays only). Smack, in fact, at the hub of Corwen's roaring night life.

Illya checked in, had a meal and went down to the saloon bar.

Trade was not booming but there was enough custom to keep the wolf from the vestibule. Three or four natives who looked like farmers were arguing in Welsh over tankards. A couple of travelling salesmen were totting up the day's total of glass beads and trade gin and plotting new skulduggery for the morrow over glasses of whisky hot. And sitting by himself at a table near the open fireplace was a character in hairy tweeds and a folkweave tie with a flannel shirt to match. He had a plate of bread and cheese and a bottle of Guinness in front of him.

Nobody paid much attention to Illya's entrance. The farmers returned his 'good evening' with a hasty 'nos da'. The two salesmen looked up, nodded briefly and returned to their figuring. The tweedy man said nothing at all.

The landlord drew a pint of bitter and Illya retired with it to a corner. Something seemed to tell him the boys could get along without his company.

All the evening his eyes kept returning to the man in the inglenook. Despite the natty country suiting he looked out of his element. He had a shaggy mop of jet black hair and his lantern-jawed face was deeply lined. His brown eyes, when he looked up to order another bottle of stout, were sad yet with a kind of burning in them. All in all Illya figured his right setting was one of those groups of arty-crafty eggheads who hang around Greenwich Village or London's Hampstead area.

At about nine o'clock he got up, muttered 'nos da' to nobody in particular and went out.

The farmers looked after him and grinned. One of them tapped the front of his head meaningly. Then they got on with their argument.

Feeling as wanted as a two-way stretch in a nunnery Illya went up to bed.

Next morning he was out bright and early, sizing up the terrain and fraternizing with the locals.

Corwen is no metropolis, being just a largish handful of grey Welsh-type houses thrown picturesquely between the mountains and the River Dee. When you've seen the main street, the cattle pens, the open-air market and the bowling greens you've been the rounds. But that was the kind of town Illya liked and he could have wished he was there with nothing more than a holiday on his mind. He could have enjoyed talking fatstock prices with the farmers and rambling around the less vertical portions of the scenery.

Around eleven o'clock, while discussing Owen Glendower with a citizen who looked as if he might have been a contemporary, he saw the shock-headed man again. He was still wearing a tweed jacked but it was ancient and bleached by sun and rain. With it he wore battered cord breeches and gumboots that were streaked with dried mud. He walked with a curious forward stoop – almost a lurch. He passed Illya, going fast, his eyes staring angrily ahead. Although he was alone he was talking in a low monotone.

'That one's an oddball,' Illya said. 'Who is he?'

'Der!' said the ancient. 'There's a pity for him. Poor fellow, indeed. It do make my throat dry to think of him.'

'I understand,' Illya said. He steered the old man into the Cader Idris. The bar, fortunately, was empty. Illya settled him at the far end and bought two pints.

The oldster raised his tankard in a fist like a withered ham. 'Davis is the name,' he quavered. 'David Davis, Pant-y-Pwll.'

'That guy out there?'

'No, man. Me! I do like to know who I am drinking with, you see.'

Illya said: 'My name's Carson. I come from Canada.'

'Canada, is it? Well, well! I had a brother went to Canada. Time of the Boer War, it was. I ain't never heard from him since.' He clucked regretfully.

'The mails are dreadful,' Illya said. 'But we were talking about the queer fellow in the gumboots.'

Davis looked at him under bushy white eyebrows. He pulled out a clay pipe, blew through it, put it between his gums. Then he went through a long pantomime of pocket patting.

'Oh, dammo!' he cackled. 'There's an old fool I am, now. Come out without my baccy pouch. And not a bit to my pipe.'

Illya sighed and went to the counter again. The bar

only carried black shag and he hoped it would poison the old bandit's declining years. He threw the packet on the table.

'Now, give,' he said.

Davis stuffed the pipe to a running commentary of 't'ck, t'cks' and 'dear, dears,' but the first swig of beer seemed to lubricate his vocal chords.

'Hugh ap Morgan,' he said. 'A foreigner like yourself, true – a Cardiff man – but a Welshman of sorts, I suppose, after all. Yes, a sad case indeed.'

Illya said: 'Let's get this straight. You're talking now about the guy outside, not some relation of yours by marriage?'

'I'm telling you, isn't it? Hugh ap Morgan of Cardiff. Bachelor of Science, University of Wales. Gaolbird!' He spat the last word out with vicious relish.

Illya held himself in. The science and gaol motif was interesting but it was too early to be optimistic. He asked patiently: 'How did he come to get in the can?'

Davis wagged his head slowly. 'Misled, he was. Those Welsh nationalists, as they do call themselves! T'ck, t'ck.'

His feelings overcame him. He had to take another drink. That meant more business with the pipe, which he had allowed to go out.

At last he went on: 'It was before the war. A big case it was, they tell me, in all the newspapers. Long sentences they all got.'

'But for what?'

'I'm telling you, isn't it? Nationalists, they were. Wanting Home Rule for Wales. So they went about burning aerodromes, blowing up bridges, and such nonsense. What they call sawbooters.'

'And this guy Morgan was one of them?'

'Ai, indeed.' He wagged his head again. 'Three years he got, because of his youth. And sentence remitted for good conduct, too.'

'But that's thirty years ago.'

Davis went on as if he hadn't heard. 'Of course he was

finished. Never got a decent job again, poor dab. Lived hand to mouth, as you might say.'

Illya said as casually as he could: 'What is he doing now?'

'Oh, he's with the lot up by Cwm Carrog. The ban-the-bomb lot, long hair and no guts.' Mr Davis spat emphatically. 'I'd ban-the-bomb 'em if I was ten years younger. And my boy Dai, Welsh Guards, dead out there in France...'

Illya bought him another pint.

'This Cwm Carrog,' he said. 'What is it?'

'Duw, man! Don't know Cwm Carrog? There's ignorance for you. A big old farm it is, right up on Berwyn, very ancient. Property of Mr Price Hughes. A gentleman. Openhandedness itself.'

'And these ban-the-bomb types work the land for him, eh?'

'Ai,' he cackled. 'Six of them it takes to do the work of two good Welshmen! And nowhere near so well, neither.'

Illya said: 'The boss is easy to please, it seems.'

'Yes, indeed. A very easy man, Mr Hughes Cwm Carrog. A shame it is the way they do take advantage of him. Loafing about half the day.'

'H'mmm! I suppose his family has been settled there since the Flood and he's past caring what happens.'

Davis shook his head. 'No, no. He bought the farm about... let's see now... about six years ago. Came from foreign parts, I'm told. London, I shouldn't wonder. A great traveller, Mr Price Hughes. That's how they can cheat him, you see. For when he is wanted, there he is – gone again. And not a sight of him for months perhaps.'

'Well, if he's so widely travelled he must be wise to these smart guys,' Illya said. 'Why doesn't he throw them out and work the place with local hands?'

'For why, man?' Mr Davis leaned close enough to give Illya a strong shot of mixed leek and beer. His rheumy eyes bulged impressively. 'Because not a man, woman or child would set foot in Cwm Carrog only in broad daylight. Haunted it is, you wouldn't believe.'

Illya grinned. 'You're a great old kidder, all right.'

If the old man had been a druid that somebody tried to kiss under the mistletoe he couldn't have been more offended. He put his gnarled hands on the table and slowly hoisted himself to his feet.

'In other places, so I am told, it is different,' he said. 'But up by here there is things we do not make a jest of. I will thank you for your beer and wish you good morning.'

He started to walk out of the bar.

'Hey! Wait,' Illya called. 'You forgot to finish your drink.'

Davis hesitated, turned, then stalked back to the table like a flouted patriarch.

'Young you are and ignorant,' he said, 'but no doubt not meaning to insult. So I will drink your beer though it do stick in my throat like gall.' The rest of the pint vanished. 'Laugh you do, now, but –' he pointed a threatening finger – 'when you have heard the thing that do wail and scream at night at Cwm Carrog, and seen the lights where none should be, a different tune you will sing, my boy.'

It made a wonderful exit. Illya almost forgot himself and clapped.

After Davis had gone he sat on, thinking. It looked as if he might have struck oil with the first drill. Totting the score he had a screwball nationalist who had done time for sabotage and looked capable of doing plenty more damage, a mysterious philanthropist who let the hired help loaf around all day, a bunch of possibly phoney nuclear disarmers, and a warranted genuine haunted house for them all to play in without fear of local peek-a-booing. And the philanthropist had a record of long absences from the home base.

The indications were that Cwm Carrog should be

inspected without delay. The wailing wonder intrigued him.

After an early lunch of Welsh lamb and all the trimmings Illya went up to his room and changed his suit for a black sweater, black windcheater and dark grey flannel slacks. A dim-out torch and a pair of rubber-soled sneakers went into the haversack he carried for form's sake.

He walked downstairs to the office and got general sailing directions from the landlord. He told him he was planning a long hike and would not be back until late next day.

The landlord made him pay for his room in advance.

# CHAPTER FIVE

IT WAS A five-mile hike to the foot of Berwyn. Illya had plenty of time, so he took it easy.

The road led through two neat little villages, all limewash and slate roofs, with shops and inns hardly distinguishable in size or appearance from the cottages. Between the hamlets he had the Dee on one side of him and woodland on the other. There was plenty to see, including a couple of patient herons on the river bank and an old forsaken church that might have been St David's original curacy.

At last, on the farther outskirts of the second village, he found himself looking up at the great rounded mass of Berwyn. Its lower slopes were thick with pines. The upper reaches were all bracken and heather, with a curious ring of firs like a crown on top. He could see a white cottage or two but nothing that looked like a sizeable farm.

He crossed an iron footbridge over a stream that might have been the Carrog and took a narrow lane which climbed up the hillside. It was bordered by high hazel hedges that made effective blinkers. Beyond the hedges and crowding close were the pines, thousands of them. Once he had got started the only sound was the crunch of flints under his boots. He felt as if he were clattering along the aisle of a cathedral.

After he had been climbing for about thirty minutes he began to wonder whether there were anything in old man Davis's tales. The green stillness was uncanny. It was as if all those damned trees were watching him... waiting for something...

He was glad when they thinned out and the hedges gave way to unmortared stone walls, letting in the wind and the sunlight. Behind the walls he could hear sheep crashing about in the miniature jungle of bracken fern. At least he hoped they were sheep. The way his nerves were, he would not have been surprised if a brace of pixies had sneaked up on him.

A few minutes more brought him to the end of the bracken belt and also to a gate in the wall. Tired of the flinty lane he pushed the gate open and trudged on among the heather, keeping the wall on his right hand side. The going was more slippery but not so hard on his aching feet.

He was now nearing the skyline. Just in case of accidents he got closer to the wall and moved forward more cautiously.

It was as well that he did. Over the shoulder of the hill and some hundreds of feet below, he saw what could only be Cwm Carrog. He dropped flat and studied the farm.

There was the usual assemblage of barns and byres, only larger than seemed usual in the neighbourhood. The farmhouse itself was a square-built grey structure, almost hidden on three sides by ancient macrocarpas. In the westering sunlight it looked unbelievably sinister. There was no sign of life in the yard or around the buildings.

Illya crawled back to the safe side of the hill and thoughtfully chewed a blade of grass. This lone expedition was beginning to look less and less attractive.

Not that he was frightened, but he was slightly out of his depth. Most of his assignments had previously been in cities, with street cars and autos making a friendly murmuring background to his investigations. It's pretty hard to take ghosts seriously under such conditions. Cwm Carrog was something else again. At the very least, if his suspicions were confirmed, he stood a fair chance of getting his teeth kicked in by Mr Price

Hughes's protégés. At worst – well, sitting there on the bare hillside in territory where folks are still apt to put out bowls of bread and milk for night-prowling goblins, he was prepared to believe that anything could happen.

The sun called it a day and sank behind a convenient mountain. Out of the pines far below a silver mist came up like a sea. A chilly night breeze began to hunt for Illya's spine through windcheater and sweater. Sheep bleated forlornly.

Illya crawled up to take another look at Cwm Carrog. It was already half submerged in the mist. He decided zero hour had come.

The journey down that hillside was to remain forever one of his major nightmares. By day it would have been easy enough but in the near-darkness he had troubles a-plenty.

At first the wall was a guide but when the last of the light had faded it became a menace. Many of the top stones had fallen among the heather. Illya found them every time, and every time he took a dive. Seen on the movies it would have been a riot, but somehow he missed the comic angle. He dared not use his torch, and if he got too far from the wall he lost his bearings. And at any minute he expected to hear the whine of a bullet heading in his direction, especially when he got down among the bracken. No matter how cautiously he trod, the stuff crackled like a forest fire with every step. He could only hope that Mr Hughes's sentries, if he had posted any, would blame the sheep.

When he was near enough to get the full bouquet of the Cwm Carrog cow byres he called a halt and sat down. He was almost through the bracken, which was now no more than knee-high. Before he started across the paddock he needed a rest.

A hint of moonrise in the east warned him that he would have to get going again. Already it was light enough for him to see ahead the outline of the farmyard wall, a shed or two and the great macrocarpas looming black against the sky.

He slipped off his walking shoes and took the sneakers and torch out of his haversack. He clipped the torch to his belt, packed the shoes in the haversack, slung the haversack over his shoulder again.

As he was lacing the sneakers he got his first jolt. It was a light – a cold greenish light about as big as a fair-sized grapefruit. And it was moving slowly along the base of the farmyard wall. Suddenly it stopped, wavered, changed direction and came uphill towards him. It moved with a queer jerky roll.

There was only one thing to do. Illya crossed his fingers, said stoutly: 'Ghosts are only your father, like Santa Claus,' and went to meet it.

It came on unsteadily, a wobbling disembodied eye, glowing weirdly.

When it got within reach Illya grabbed.

His hand blotted out the light. Closed on something hard and smooth. The thing stopped, went dead under his grasp.

Wriggling closer so that he got it under cover of his body Illya fumbled with his free hand for the torch and pressed the button.

The beam stabbed briefly, flooding a small tortoise. Some humourist had thought up the idea of painting its shell with phosphorescent paint. Illya let it go and lay still. After a minute or so a puzzled crustacean wobbled off to spread panic and despondency elsewhere.

Illya pressed on, much heartened. The *tête-à-tête* had not only put paid to David Davis's fairy tales. It had also proved that whatever funny business was going on at Cwm Carrog had human brains behind it. In a way Illya was disappointed. If luminous tortoises were the best the Price Hughes faction could do they didn't come in the same class with some of the gangs he had bucked.

Between the edge of the bracken and the yard wall

there was a short stretch of open turf. Illya covered it very slowly like Napoleon's army. On the belly.

Once safe in the shadow of the wall he straightened up and felt his way back to where it joined the lane wall. He tucked his haversack away in the angle, where he could find it again. It was too awkward to lug around on his sleuthing. On the other hand he did not fancy the long hike back to Corwen in sneakers.

Getting a toe-hold among the rough stones he pulled himself up and with a hand cupped over the lens of the dim-out torch examined the top of the yard wall for possible alarm wire. There was none. A second later he was in the yard.

By this time the moon was well up. He thanked his joss that the sky was cloudy. A clear night would have been fatal. He hugged the wall for a space, getting his bearings. Fifty feet away was a Dutch barn, half full of hay. If he could make that safely it was an easy step, all in shadow, to the shelter of the macrocarpas round the house. Offering up a prayer against shepherd dogs and watchmen, as soon as the moon passed behind a cloud drift he sprinted.

It was then that he got his second taste of the amenities of Cwm Carrog. And this time it shook him.

He had just made it to the barn and was cuddling the hay when it came – a ghastly sound that began with a low sobbing wail and rose to a long-drawn-out hysterical scream with insane laughter in it. It sounded as if a dozen cougars had sat down suddenly on the same number of electric stoves. Illya could feel every one of the hairs on his scalp rising individually and icy fingers played along his backbone.

The cry died away into broken moaning. Illya strained his ears but nobody in the house seemed to be paying any attention. Not a light went on. The only sound now was the whisper of the wind through the barn. He got a grip on himself and went on, picking his steps carefully. He did not want to tangle with trip wires or spring guns and Mr Price Hughes was evidently a considerable joker.

At last he was on the farther side of the trees, looking up at the house. He could see six windows, three up and three down, all shuttered tightly.

He scouted along to the left and found himself at the back of the premises. Here, too, the windows were close-shuttered. The blackness was relieved only by one of the fiery tortoises, which was pottering about moodily. Illya tried the solid-looking door. It had no latch or handle. Nothing but some kind of patent lock that fitted flush. He ran his hand over the surface of the door. It was cold metal.

Suddenly the howling started again, this time apparently right overhead. Illya looked up. There was nothing to see but the dark oblongs of the windows, like sightless eyes, and the denser shadow of the overhanging eaves.

The noise went through the same routine, a crescendo shriek dying away into sobbing. When it stopped there was no sound but the wind in the trees.

Illya grinned. He had got the answer to Winnie the Wailer though he couldn't quite place her hideout. That could come later.

He was working around the end of the third wall to the front of the house when he heard a car approaching. Across a widish gravel drive, facing the main entrance, there was a clump of laurels. He nipped among them quickly.

The purr of the engine got louder. Headlights swept the drive. The car, a big sedan, stopped. A man got out, held the rear door wide. After an interval two more men appeared.

The door of the house opened. Light streamed out brightly, enabling Illya to get a look at the new arrivals.

The man who had got out of the driver's seat was a stocky, broad-shouldered character, clean-shaven, with horn-rimmed spectacles and a mean expression. The second had a skinny frame, nutcracker nose and chin, and a high-domed skull with just a fringe of white hair above the ears. The third man was Hugh ap Morgan.

Illya took a sub-miniature camera from the inside pocket of his windcheater. It had a special lens and was loaded with supersensitive 16 mm. film capable of getting pictures in almost total darkness. Illya checked with his finger tips on the Braille-type indicator that the focus was set at twelve feet. Then he photographed the group and then each man in turn.

Morgan went around to the boot of the car, unlocked it and dragged out two heavy suitcases. He took one in each hand and lugged them with some difficulty into the hall. The other two men hurried after him and the door swung shut.

It opened again a minute later. The stocky man reappeared, got into the car and drove it round to the yard.

Illya decided to call it a night. He had plenty to think about and there was no use straining his luck.

Getting out of Cwm Carrog was no trick. He went out the front way – along the edge of the drive to the lane – then walked uphill to the place where he had left the haversack. He picked up the sack but left his sneakers on. When he had walked about half a mile he changed them for his shoes, climbed over the lone wall and nested down among the bracken for the remainder of the night.

At first light he worked his cramped muscles into a state approaching normal, climbed the hill to the ring of pines and hiked down into Corwen from the other side.

Illya timed his arrival at the hotel for a late breakfast. Since he had to pay for it he thought he might as well eat it. Afterwards he had a hot bath and changed into more civilized clothes. Then he hung a sign outside his bedroom door: 'Do not disturb,' and went to work on the film.

At noon he left the hotel and hunted out David Davis. He found the old man sitting hopefully on a bench outside a small beerhouse. He took him inside, propped him against the bar with a pint in front of him, and produced one of the prints he had made that morning. It showed the thin man with the nutcracker features.

Illya said: 'Do you know this man?'

Mr Davis cackled. 'Der! There's a joker you are. Making me tell you all about him – and all the time you do know him well enough to carry his picture. Yes, indeed. Mr Price Hughes himself. A speaking likeness.'

Illya put a pound note in his willing palm. He said, without optimism: 'Forget I ever mentioned him.'

Down at the post office he met an official obviously fitted for bigger things. Without asking too many questions he got an ex-directory number in Newport and handed Illya the receiver.

Blodwen's voice said: 'How're they coming, my Russian cousin?'

'Like gold,' he said happily. 'Has Solo arrived?'

'He's here now – punishing my Scotch. Want to talk to him?'

'Not right now. Tell him I'm sending some pictures by special delivery. I want them checked.'

'The hunch came off?'

'And how! I've found a bunch of weirdies living the simple life behind bullet-proof doors – with aeolian harps and livestock in gorgeous Technicolour to keep the locals at bay.'

She said: 'And what the hell is a you-know-what harp?'

'Oh, that! It's a quaint gadget of piano wires or guitar strings. You fix it some place where the wind can blow through it and it sounds like slaughter on Tenth Avenue. Just the thing for the baby's nursery.'

There was a pause. Then Solo's voice came over the wire. He said: 'Nice work, Illya. But play it cool.'

Illya grinned into a fly-specked mirror tilted above the switchboard. 'I won't lift a finger till the gang arrives. Just a unit in one great army, that's me.'

He put a bunch of prints into a distinctively coloured

envelope, gave the postal official some instructions, and walked out into the sunshine.

# CHAPTER SIX

ILLYA POTTERED around the town for the rest of the day, looking in at the cattle market, buying picture postcards, sharing the joys and sorrows of the grand-dads on the bowling green. He let it be generally understood that he was a footloose Canadian with no more on his mind than a few days' relaxation. David Davis might have his own ideas, but as long as the free beer held out, Illya didn't think he would talk.

Around dusk he went back to the hostel. The landlord said there had been no messages for him. He ate a leisurely dinner and spent the rest of the evening in the bar. Neither David Davis nor Hugh ap Morgan showed up. At ten o'clock he shut himself in the telephone box in the lobby and dialled Blodwen's number.

Solo answered the call.

Illya asked: 'Did you get the pictures?'

'I did, and I've run a check. The old man is Price Hughes, all right. He seems to be a professional eccentric but otherwise his reputation is unblemished. He has more money than Fort Knox and he spends it on good works. Apart from the nut colony you've uncovered he heads an organization for reforming ex-convicts, which he runs from his apartment in Newport Street, London'

'In Soho? That's an odd address for a philanthropist.'

'I told you. He's an eccentric.'

'Sure.' Illya sounded unconvinced. 'What about the other two?'

'The guy in the cheaters is one of his strayed lambs. A

simple soul called Rafferty with a list of convictions from here to Glasgow. Grievous bodily harm, shooting with intent, mugging – you name it, he's done it. He's worked as a strong-arm man in race-track protection, organized prostitution and smuggling. But now, he claims, he's seen the light. He's been in the clear since he came out of Dartmoor a year ago.'

'And Morgan?'

'That,' said Solo, 'is the jackpot question. You know some of the answers. He got mixed up with politics and did three years for arson. Maybe that's how he got in touch with Price Hughes. But here's the interesting thing. Before he got into trouble he was in line for a professorship in the University of Wales. It seems he was some kind of boy genius with a special bent for electronics. According to my sources he was tinkering about with one of the first experimental computers when the blow fell.'

'Intriguing,' Illya murmured.

'Wait. It gets better. He did his time in Wakefield, where a prisoner gets a reasonable choice of studies. Morgan elected to work in the printing shop. He knew he was washed up academically and he wanted to learn a trade.

'When he was released the Ministry of Labour found him a place with a firm that specializes in fine printing and engraving, but it didn't work out. He got restless and quit. He joined the army, volunteered for special duties, and was next heard of in one of the hush-hush outfits, forging documents for the Resistance movements.

'After the war he drifted from job to job and finally dropped out of sight. He wasn't heard of again until six years ago when Price Hughes bought his farm. Morgan was the first man he hired.'

Illya said: 'Well, well! Things begin to add up.'

'They do, indeed. There's not much doubt that the farm is the centre of operations. I think it's time we stopped the presses.'

'High time,' said Illya. 'But getting near them will be quite a trick.'

He replaced the receiver and went up to bed.

At nine o'clock next morning he walked into the dining-room for breakfast. And there, working earnestly through a plate of ham and eggs, sat Blodwen. She was wearing a suit of cheap tweed with a chain-store jumper. Her black hair was combed lankly and she wore all the wrong kinds of make-up.

She looked up uninterestedly when Illya walked in, then resumed her assault on the ham.

He took the chair opposite from her. The waitress brought him a bowl of cereal.

'Nice morning,' he said.

Blodwen scowled. 'Dim Saesneg,' she answered with her mouth full.

'I beg your pardon?'

'The lady do say she don't speak no English,' the waitress interpreted. 'A Welsh lady she is,' she added unnecessarily.

'"Lady" is right,' Illya said as a heavy brogue landed on his shin. He got his revenge by making the cereal really audible.

He had got to the toast and marmalade stage when Blodwen brought out a packet of cigarettes. She lit one, then started to transfer the others to a case. Somehow she fumbled the job. The case made a clatter on the table and the cigarettes spread over the floor.

Illya bent down to pick them up. So did Blodwen. Her hair brushed his cheek and he liked it.

She whispered: 'The little red schoolhouse. In half an hour.'

When the cigarettes had all been retrieved she straightened up, muttering grudging thanks in Welsh and walked out. She left a threepenny piece by her plate for the waitress. Illya thought it was wonderful how quickly she had picked up the customs of the country. He didn't know then that she was born in Wrexham.

He allowed her time to get clear of the hotel, then went down to the lobby and wasted fifteen minutes talking to the receptionist.

There are several schools in Corwen but he thought he knew the one Blodwen meant. It stood only about a hundred yards from the Cader Idris and it wasn't red. He strolled along to it.

She was standing outside the playground gate, nursing the poodle. As Illya approached she turned to her right and began walking. He followed at a discreet distance as she cut down a long, narrow street of workmen's cottages. An old Austin twelve was parked at the kerb outside a little general store. She climbed in and waited for him to come up. He opened the door, settled himself beside her and said: 'Surprise, surprise! When did you get in?'

'Last night. Solo had the thought that you needed a hand.' She let in the clutch and headed for the open country. The poodle snuggled into her lap and went to sleep.

'And the fancy dress?'

She laughed. 'I was out at Cwm Carrog bright and early this morning, before you were out of bed. Just to see what I could pick up, as you might say.

'As you know, it's a two-storey house with entrances front and back. The main entrance, facing on to the drive, has double doors. There's a single door at the back. They're faced with steel painted like wood and all the windows have steel shutters.

'Round the back of the cobbled yard there are two barns – one Dutch, one modern brick – a brick stable and a cowshed. All normal as far as I could judge. Built on to the stable is a garage for two cars. They were both in when I got there. One is a big Vauxhall, number LP0094, finished black. The other is a Mini-van, grey, number XL4454.'

She took a notebook from the glove compartment,

tore out a leaf and passed it to him. 'There's the layout of the buildings.'

Illya studied it carefully. He said: 'Did you get into the house?'

'No. A man working in the garage stopped me. A big guy in overalls. He wore horn-rimmed glasses and spoke like a Londoner.'

'Rafferty,' Illya said.

'Yes? Well, I talked Welsh at him till he was in a flat spin. He told me to wait, went over to the back door of the house and knocked. Your chum Morgan came to the door. They talked for a few seconds and I think Morgan got suspicious. He called me over and started shooting questions at me.

'I told him I was starting a new job at Rhys's farm and had lost my way.

'He checked and cross-checked every angle – how long I'd been in the dairymaid business, where I'd come from, which Labour Exchange had sent me to Rhys's – but all so it seemed like ordinary Welsh curiosity. Finally he seemed satisfied and gave me my route. But the other chap walked right back to the lane with me to see that I took it.'

Illya asked: 'You didn't see anything of Price Hughes – the old man?'

'No. Nobody but Morgan and this other fellow. Didn't you tell Solo there were six men up there?'

'Don't quote me on it,' Illya said. 'All I saw was three. But if Davis is right, there are seven – counting Price Hughes himself.'

'That's – Blast! what does that fool think he's doing?'

A big combine harvester was backing slowly out of a side lane only a few yards ahead, blocking the entire road. Blodwen had to jam the brakes on hard to avoid a collision. She said furiously: 'What the hell is he trying to do? He can't possibly turn in that space.'

She wound down the side-window, leaned out and

loosed a torrent of Welsh. The combine driver grinned back stupidly.

Illya was looking through the rear window. He said: 'Oh, oh! Don't bother. We've got company.'

A black Vauxhall saloon was coming up behind them, fast. Its number plate read LP0094.

Illya's hand went to the P38 under his left armpit, then dropped away. Rafferty was sitting beside the Vauxhall's driver, cuddling a Thompson sub-machine gun. And his finger was on the trigger. He could have put a burst through the Austin's rear before Illya's pistol had cleared its holster.

The black car came to a halt about ten feet behind the Austin. The driver climbed out and took up a position where he could cover both Blodwen and Illya with his wartime-issue Sten gun. He was a sullen-looking teenager, dressed in jeans and a check shirt. His hair hung Beatle-style to his unwashed neck. A CND badge was pinned to the breast pocket of his shabby jacket.

Rafferty walked forward, pulled open the car doors and stood back a pace, tommy-gun at the ready.

'Get out,' he said. 'And don't try anything.'

He motioned to the teenager with the snout of the gun. 'Give 'em a rub-down.'

The grubby youth cradled the Sten in the crook of his arm and came round the bonnet of the car. There was a glint in his unpleasant eyes that said he was going to enjoy searching the girl.

Illya said: 'I'll make it easy for us all.' He took the P38 from its holster and threw it on the grass verge.

'You think I'm daft?' Rafferty sneered. 'Turn round and put your hands on the roof of the jalopy.'

'How can I?' Blodwen demanded. 'I'm holding my dog.'

'Well, put the bloody thing on the ground,' he said. 'Unless you want me to wring its neck. Now come on. Get weaving.'

She obeyed. The poodle crouched by her feet, making

high-pitched whimpering sounds. She was a pup who liked her comfort.

The teenager ran his hands down Illya's body, patting at chest and hips. "E's clean,' he announced.

'Which is more than could be said for you,' Illya murmured. 'Did you ever try taking a bath, my smelly friend?'

'Ah! button yer lip.'

He moved on to the girl. This time his examination was more lingering. Blodwen shuddered. When his grimy fingers curled near her pelvis she revolted. Her brogue-shod foot lashed back viciously.

The youth screamed and bent double, clutching his groin.

Rafferty laughed.

'Serve you right, you bleeding little creep,' he said. 'You asked for it.' Then his voice hardened. 'All right, you two mugs. You're going for a ride.'

He marched them to the Vauxhall and opened the rear door. 'In!' he ordered. And to Illya: 'You first, then the dame.'

He wedged himself in beside them, the tommy-gun's snout uncomfortably close to Blodwen's midriff. He warned again: 'Don't try anything. I'm liable to get nervous.'

Illya said: 'You should take something for it. Where are we going, or shouldn't I ask?'

'The boss wants to see you. Now belt up!'

The teenager got behind the steering wheel and made a thumbs-up signal through the windscreen. The man on the combine-harvester made an answering gesture. The big machine started up with a jolt and lumbered back the way it had come. The teenager put his foot on the accelerator and the Vauxhall nosed forward.

After a few miles the car turned right off the main road and jolted through a fir plantation along a rutted track that was hard on the springs. The track ended in a farm gate and beyond there were outbuildings and a grey house flanked by macrocarpas.

Illya said: 'Ah! the old homestead.'

The driver sounded the car horn twice. Morgan, wearing overalls and gumboots, came out of the brick barn and opened the gate. The Vauxhall rolled through into the yard of Cwm Carrog and stopped by the back door of the house. The driver slid from behind the wheel, picked up the Sten gun and opened the door on Illya's side of the car.

Rafferty waggled the tommy-gun and said: 'Out!'

Illya stepped down, followed by Blodwen. While the teenager kept his gun on them Rafferty walked forward and opened the house door. He said: 'In here,' and stood aside for them to pass.

They found themselves in a stone-flagged, white-washed kitchen, furnished with a long Welsh dresser, a plain deal table and six straight-backed chairs. An old-fashioned iron range took up most of one end of the room. At the other end there was an open door. Rafferty motioned them towards it.

He herded them through and along a passage that opened into a wide, oak-panelled hall. Heavy gilt frames on the walls held pictures of somebody's ancestors. There was a sombre grandfather clock with a tick that sounded like the rap of a hammer on a coffin lid. A broad staircase with dark oak banisters led up to the first floor.

Morgan came through from the kitchen, knocked on a door at the right-hand side of the hall and flung it open. He said: 'They're here.'

The bright, airy room could have been the parlour in a vicarage. It had cream-washed walls, high and well-proportioned, a moulded ceiling with a pattern of wreaths and cherubs, and a fireplace that might have been Adam. The chairs and sofa had loose covers of flowered cretonne somewhat in need of laundering. High leaded windows looked out on to flower beds and a green expanse of lawn.

Price Hughes was sitting at a Victorian oval table in the exact centre of the room. He wore a rusty black coat, grey striped trousers, a stiff white collar with oversize wings that exposed his adam's apple, and an old-fashioned black cravat. His feet were encased incongruously in tartan carpet slippers that had black metal fasteners like belt buckles. Apart from the slippers, he could have been an old-time market-place medicine faker.

He sat huddled forward in the ladder-back chair with his hands on the table, gnarled fingers interlaced. His slate-grey eyes were as full of human kindness as a horned toad.

He said without preamble: 'Who are you, and why do you persist in pestering me?' He spoke in a queer harsh whisper.

Blodwen laughed. 'That's rich,' she said. 'It seems to me the pestering has been all on your side. Here we are, out for a quiet morning ride, and suddenly your hoodlums set on us with enough artillery to finish a war. This we should enjoy?'

'Morning ride, my foot!' Rafferty interjected. 'The bloke was carrying a Luger.'

'A P38, my friend,' Illya corrected mildly. 'There's a difference.'

The old man made an impatient gesture. 'That's enough! Rafferty, hand your weapon to Mr Morgan and get back to your duties. One guard is sufficient.'

He waited until the door had closed behind the strong-arm man. Then he said to Illya: 'Let us have no more prevarication. You have been making inquiries about Cwm Carrog ever since you arrived in Corwen. The girl was here early this morning with some trumped-up story of finding employment in the neighbourhood. That, frankly, I find as incredible as your claim to be a Canadian tourist.'

'Then what's your guess?' Blodwen asked.

'I will tell you.' His knuckles cracked as he pushed

53

himself to his feet. 'You are two typically clumsy agents of the United Network Command of Law and Enforcement.'

'In that case,' said Illya, 'you know exactly why we are here. U.N.C.L.E. doesn't approve of naughty people who make their own money.'

'And you innocents were sent to stop us?' The old man emitted a graveyard sound that was probably intended to signify amusement. 'You had the audacity to pit yourselves against Thrush? That was unfortunate – for you.'

'That's the way it looks,' Illya admitted. 'But don't bank on it. You might be disappointed.'

Price Hughes shook his head. 'You have been a nuisance,' he said. 'No doubt you have sent a certain amount of information back to your headquarters. But it was useless. U.N.C.L.E. can do nothing to stop us now. We have worked here undisturbed for almost six years. Our mission is practically completed. Even without your intervention we should have left Cwm Carrog within the next week. Nothing remains but to dismantle the plant. You have merely made it necessary to expedite our departure.'

Blodwen said: 'That doesn't make sense. None of your phoney notes appeared until your man turned up stone-cold dead in the market. What have you been doing for the past six years? Just practising?'

He cackled again. 'You see?' he said. 'You don't think things through. We are not common forgers. It was never our intention to circulate the currency piece-meal. During our operation paper to the face value of one hundred million pounds has been transported from Britain and lodged in secret depositories throughout Europe and the United States. Soon it will be released – not by degrees but in a sudden flood. And the result will be world-wide chaos.'

He sank back into his chair, his eyes suddenly dull. 'Take them away,' he said to Morgan. 'Lock them up.'

Illya said: 'One moment. Just to satisfy my professional curiosity, how did you achieve such perfect reproductions?' He put real regret into his voice. 'That I should like to have seen.'

Price Hughes drummed his fingers on the table top, considering. Then he replied: 'There is no reason why you shouldn't. It can make no difference now.' He looked up at Morgan. 'Show them your handiwork before you put them away.'

Morgan said with the pride of an artist: 'It will be a pleasure.'

# CHAPTER SEVEN

THEY WENT back into the hall. Morgan whistled and Rafferty came from the kitchen at the double. Morgan handed him the tommy-gun and said: 'Keep them covered.'

He walked across to the grandfather clock, opened the glass door over the clock face, set the hands to twelve o'clock and stepped back. The clock whirred and swung away from the wall on oiled hinges, revealing a short brick corridor that opened into a brilliantly lit room. There was an acrid odour of printing ink and acid. An electric motor crooned in a high register.

Morgan led the way through the corridor. Rafferty with the gun brought up the rear.

Batteries of neon tubes in the high ceiling flooded the room with an effect approximating natural light. The place looked more like an electricity generating station than a printing plant. At one end, covering almost the entire wall, there was an ebonite panel where red, green and yellow lamps glowed and winked like small circular eyes and needles quivered against white dials. The humming sound came from a single long, low-built machine which extended down the centre of the room. It was entirely enclosed by gunmetal-grey panels in some form of plastic and at intervals along its length there were shielded observation peepholes. Towards the farther end there was a domed extrusion like the gun turret of a bomber.

Stacked high against one wall of the room were flat

rectangular packages that Illya guessed contained banknote paper. Along the other wall were ranged crates bound with thin metal strip.

There was only one man in the room. He was sitting at a desk near the machine, studying a set of graphs. He wore a white laboratory coat over an open green shirt and cavalry twill slacks. His hands bore the yellow stain of acid. He looked up, did a double-take when he saw the poodle in Blodwen's arms, then returned to his work without a word.

Illya said: 'Well, well! So this is the instant-currency plant. How does it work?'

'It's simple, really.' Hugh ap Morgan spoke deprecatingly, in the way inventors do. 'It was just a matter of applying automation to the job. The old-time forger was too slow – and too uncertain. It is not easy to copy a note by hand. The best of craftsmen made mistakes. And photo-reproduction had its drawbacks. There was the matter of numbering, for instance.' His voice took on the singsong intonation of the North Welshman as he warmed to his lecture.

'Now we have cut out all that. My press works on the continuous process, and it is completely automatic. There is no place for human error. The press does everything – and does it perfectly. Only the paper is not quite right – and that is not our fault. It is made elsewhere, unfortunately. The heart of the machine, and the first stage, is the computer.'

He took a pound note from his trousers pocket and called to the man in the white coat. 'Mr Jones, if you please, will you come and demonstrate?'

Jones got up from the desk, went to the ebonite control panel and made adjustments. He returned, took the note from Morgan's hand and crossed to the head of the machine.

Morgan said: 'Now watch.'

Jones fitted the note into what looked like the darkslide of an old-fashioned plate camera. He dropped the slide into a slot and turned a switch. The hum of the electric motor rose to a higher pitch. Lights on the control panel danced crazily.

Morgan said: 'The computer is scanning and absorbing every detail of the note. The knowledge will now be fed to the etching, printing and numbering sections. Now come with me.'

He led them to the far end of the machine. They saw brand-new pound notes stacking themselves with lightning rapidity into a glass receiver.

Morgan signalled to the man in the white coat. The sound of the motor died to its original low humming. The stream of notes stopped.

Morgan picked up the top dozen from the pile and splayed them fanwise. 'You see? They are numbered individually – but not consecutively. When they go into circulation there'll be no chance of putting a warning out to block a series. The numbering is quite random.'

'Very clever,' Illya said. 'It's almost a pity your boss will be picked up before the scheme has time to get under way.'

'If he is,' Morgan retorted surprisingly. 'it won't matter. He's expendable, like the rest of us. What gave you the idea he was heading the operation?' He motioned towards the door. 'You've seen all there is to see. It's time I put you to bed.'

As they passed the man in the white coat he grinned and invited: 'Come again.'

'We should live so long,' Blodwen said gloomily.

They went out through the hall and the kitchen into the yard.

Rafferty asked: 'The usual?' and Morgan said: 'Where else?' He led the way across the yard to the brick-built barn and opened the door. There was a warm smell of cows and hay. The concrete floor was newly washed.

A heavy oak door was let into the far wall of the barn. Morgan unlocked it and stood aside. Rafferty said: 'In!' It seemed to be his favourite word. He jabbed Illya in the back with the muzzle of the tommy-gun. Illya stumbled over the threshold, almost sending Blodwen sprawling. The door slammed behind them and the key turned in the lock.

Blodwen looked around her. She said: 'Charming, though perhaps a little austere.'

The chamber in which they were standing measured about ten feet by eight. Walls, ceiling and floor were of smooth concrete and the inside surface of the door was a sheet of steel. There were no windows. The only light came from a low-wattage bulb behind a thick glass cover set into the ceiling. There was no furniture of any kind. The air smelled cold and damp.

Illya ran his hand down the wall. His fingers came away wet. He said: 'If they keep us here long they won't need to send in the execution squad. We'll die of pneumonia.'

'You say the nicest things,' Blodwen told him. 'I like a man who looks on the bright side.' She rubbed the poodle's head. 'I wish I had some food for this animal. The poor little soul must be starving.'

Illya looked at his wristwatch. 'It's half after one. I don't think they intend to bring us lunch, somehow.'

'Ah, well! We mustn't expect too much. After all, like the man said, we're expendable.'

He glanced at her, puzzled. 'You seem to be taking things remarkably lightly.'

She shrugged. 'Not much point in doing anything else, is there? The next move is up to them.' She took off her jacket, folded it as a cushion and settled herself as comfortably as could be expected in a corner of the cell. She said: 'I wish that little horror in the blue jeans hadn't taken my handbag. I'm dying for a cigarette. You wouldn't have one, I suppose?'

'I'm afraid not.'

'Never mind. It's a killing habit.' She clasped the poodle tight and closed her eyes. Illya, looking down on her, thought she seemed unbelievably young.

She slept for three hours. Then Illya shook her gently. She sat up, instantly alert. 'What is it?'

'Somebody's coming.'

She listened, heard the faint sound of approaching footsteps. 'Good!' she said. 'It's time Dolly did her parlour trick. Let's hope it comes off.'

She unbuckled the poodle's jewelled collar and tugged at it. The buckle came away from the strap, exposing a length of fine steel wire. She shook out her jacket and spread it over her knees, putting her hands holding the wire beneath it. As the key turned in the lock she slumped over, suddenly the picture of dejection.

The door opened and the teenager came in. He carried a tray with two tin mugs of tea and a plate of sandwiches. 'You better make the most of it,' he said. 'It's all you'll get tonight.' He looked at the girl huddled in the corner. 'What's wrong with her, then?'

She gasped: 'I'm ill.'

'Too bad,' he sneered. 'I'm no bloody doctor.'

She said painfully: 'There must be someone...'

'Not here, there ain't. You'll just have to suffer.'

She looked up, pleading. 'Well, can you give me a cigarette? Maybe that will ease the pain.'

'Yes, I can manage that.' He took a packet of Players from his jacket pocket and threw a cigarette into her lap. She picked it up, put it in her mouth, and put her hand back under the jacket, shuddering as if with cold. She said weakly: 'I don't have a light.'

'A proper little nuisance, aren't you?' He produced a lighter, flicked it into flame and bent over her.

Her hands came up swiftly, expertly twisting the wire around his neck. He made a retching sound. His tongue came out and his eyes bulged. Illya completed the demolition with a swinging right to the jaw. The teenager fell forward in a heap.

Blodwen wriggled from under him and grabbed the poodle, which was yapping shrill encouragement. She said: Nice work, pardner. Now all ashore that's going ashore. I think we've outlived our welcome.'

They raced to the outer door of the barn. Illya peered out cautiously. The yard was empty. He said: 'The boundary wall is on your left, about a hundred yards away. Keep low and sprint for it. The quicker we're among the bracken, the better.'

Blodwen tucked the poodle under her arm like a parcel. She said: 'Right, men! Hold on to your hats.'

They ran.

They got across the yard unseen and scrambled over the wall. They were fifty yards up the hillside when there came a rattle of machine-gun fire and a bullet sang past Illya's ear like a hornet. He looked back over his shoulder. Rafferty was pounding across the yard from the house. Behind him were Morgan and the man in the white coat. Another man was racing towards the hill at a different angle.

Illya said: 'Keep going. Our only chance is to lose them in the high fern.'

'You believe in fairies, too?' Blodwen panted.

Another burst of slugs thudded into the ground, uncomfortably close. She said, still struggling upward: 'He's getting the range. It won't be long now.'

'Save your breath,' Illya advised. 'And try to zigzag.'

She said: 'I haven't got enough troubles?'

They forged on, the stiff bracken stems whipping and cutting at their faces. The growth was getting thicker, affording them more protection, but the going got tougher by the minute. To add to their difficulties the short grass beneath the fern was slippery as a ballroom floor.

Illya risked another backward glance. Rafferty, legs straddled, was steadying himself for another burst. As he brought the tommy-gun up to position, a shot cracked from somewhere higher up the hill. Rafferty stumbled and went down slowly as if he were praying.

Three more shots came from the hidden marksman.

The man in the white coat screamed and clutched at his shoulder.

'Dear me!' Illya said mildly. 'Now where did the Seventh Cavalry spring from?'

'Whoever it is, he's tucked away somewhere above us and to the right,' Blodwen said. 'We'd better try to reach him.'

The gun cracked again. It sounded nearer. Illya said: 'Sit tight. He's coming this way.'

They waited, listening to the sounds of somebody moving through the fern. After a while the bracken above them parted.

Solo said: 'Having fun, my children?'

Blodwen smiled prettily. 'How nice of you to drop in. Do you come here often?'

'Only for the shooting. And by the way, you'd better have this. He handed Illya a Luger pistol.

Illya hefted it, testing the balance. He said gravely: 'Thank you. I was feeling a little undressed.' He sighted and pressed the trigger. A spurt of rock flew from the wall an inch from where Morgan was crouching. The Welshman's answering shots went wild.

'Next time,' Illya said. He aimed carefully and fired. Morgan pitched sideways and lay still.

'That leaves one,' Blodwen commented.

'If he has any sense, he'll keep going,' Solo said. 'I think it's time we moved in.'

'Too late!' Illya pointed to the grey bulk of Cwm Carrog. Smoke was pouring from the upper windows. And as they watched the roof collapsed in a sheet of flame. Almost in the same instant a black Vauxhall nosed out of the garage and headed for the main drive at speed.

'There goes Mr Price Hughes,' said Blodwen. 'Ah, well! Back to the drawing board.'

# CHAPTER EIGHT

SOLO AND ILLYA parked the Cortina in an all-night garage off Leicester Square. They walked up Charing Cross Road past the Underground station, crossed the road and entered ill-lit Newport Street. About half-way down on the right-hand side a scarlet neon sign read 'Gloriana. Dancing.'

Illya looked at it doubtfully. He asked: 'You sure this is the place?'

'That's what the number says,' Solo confirmed. 'The flat is on the first floor. There's probably another way in.'

A painted girl in a uniform of sequins eyed them from the doorway of the club. She switched on a mechanical smile and said: 'You coming in, boys? Lots of girls and all very friendly.' She looked about fifteen.

Illya said: 'Not to-night. We're busy.'

'Some other time, eh?' She returned indifferently to buffing her finger nails with a grubby handkerchief.

A plain street door adjoined the club. Above the letter-box a square board carried the message in gold letters: 'New Beginnings, first floor. Go straight up.'

'This is it,' Solo said. He pressed against the wood. The door held firm.

Illya crossed the street, looked up and came back again. He said: 'No lights showing anywhere.'

'Fine!' Solo took a length of metal from his pocket, inserted it into the keyhole and twisted. The lock clicked back. They slipped quickly into the musty-smelling hallway. Solo shut the door and pressed the button of his torch. The beam played over walls that needed repainting, and came to rest on lino-covered stairs.

They stood listening for a few moments. Only the sounds of traffic outside disturbed the stillness. They went forward cautiously.

The stairs ended at a short landing. A door in the wall was marked. 'New Beginnings. Knock and enter.'

'We won't bother to knock,' Solo said. He tried the handle. It turned in his hand and the door opened. Reflected light from the uncurtained windows lit the room greyly. It was a small office, furnished only with a plain table, a filing cabinet and a couple of hard-seated chairs. A calendar from a religious publishing house hung over the filing cabinet. Above the mantelpiece of the empty grate there was a text that promised: 'All things are possible to him that believeth.'

Solo went over to the filing cabinet. It was unlocked. He went through the drawers rapidly. They contained nothing but case-histories of pathetically inept villains.

He said: 'There's no joy here. It's obviously where Price Hughes interviewed the customers. Let's try up top.'

Another stairway almost opposite the office led up to a white-enamelled door. It had two locks that made Solo wince. He said: 'These are going to be difficult.' While Illya held the torch he worked on them with picks of a dozen designs. After five minutes he stood back, defeated.

Illya said consolingly: 'You could always try a ferret.'

'It could come to that. But we'll try brute force first.' Solo lifted his right foot and turned the rubber heel on the shoe. He removed two plastic capsules from the cavity underneath, pinched the ends to point and inserted them in the keyholes of the locks. He said: 'Stand clear,' flicked a cigarette lighter and tipped the flame to the capsules. They went 'phutt!' like damp squibs. The door sagged and swung open.

The torch beam lit up a hall in almost shocking

contrast to the office below. The floor was covered with thick carpet in a rich deep blue. The walls, like the door, were enamelled white, with panels of glowing tapestry. A Regency sofa-table held a bowl of exquisite Chinese workmanship.

Illya said: 'It looks like this is where the New Beginnings really start. You know, like charity begins at home.'

Three doors opened off the hall. Solo pushed through the first, then whipped out fast. He pulled the Luger from his shoulder holster and flattened against the wall, signalling to Illya to douse the torch.

In the darkness Illya moved silently over the carpet to his side. 'What gives?' he whispered.

'There's a gang in there,' Solo breathed. 'About a dozen of them.'

They waited tensely. Minutes passed, but the silence remained unbroken.

Illya whispered: 'They're keeping mighty quiet. Should we stir them up?'

'Hold it!' Solo's hand moved carefully up the door jamb, found the light switch and depressed it. A soft pink glow flooded through the doorway. Nothing else happened.

Solo stepped forward, gun ready, and stared into an empty bathroom. Then he burst out laughing. 'Brother!' he exclaimed. 'How kinky can you get?'

The four walls and ceiling were covered completely with small squares of mirror glass which reflected his figure a thousand times. It was those images, seen like shadows in the light from the torch, which had made him bolt for cover.

Illya said wonderingly: 'Now I've seen everything. Will you look at the marble bath-tub and the gold- plated dolphin taps?'

'*And* the celluloid ducks,' Solo grinned. 'Imagine the pride of Cwm Carrog sitting there, playing with those.'

'Must I? Let's find something less Freudian.'

The second door opened into the sitting-room. Solo crossed to the windows, pulled the heavy velvet curtains and switched on a standard lamp. Like the hall, the room was decorated and furnished richly and with good taste. Two or three antique pieces blended comfortably with the modern armchairs and long settee. A Steinway piano stood at an angle to the windows. The walls were hung with Dürer engravings in slim black frames.

Solo looked at the smooth, meticulously arranged cushions on the chairs and settee. He walked to the piano and ran a finger over its surface. It came away with a thin film of dust. He said: 'It looks as though nobody has been in here for weeks.'

'Or as if everything has been stage-managed,' Illya amended. 'The place is *too* tidy.'

He pulled open the drawers of a Georgian bureau. They were all empty. 'You see? It isn't reasonable. Everybody leaves a few papers around, even if they are only old bills.'

'Could be,' Solo admitted. 'We'll take a look at the bedroom.'

Their search there was equally unrewarding. The gold satin cover on the bed was uncreased. The pillows and sheets beneath it might have been new. Silver-backed toilet articles stood in geometrically perfect array on the walnut dressing-table. Only a row of hangers occupied the wardrobe. There was not even a smell of mothballs.

Solo said: 'You're right. It doesn't add up. Somebody's tried to arrange the impression that the old man's flown the coop. But it's too perfect.' He pointed to the silver gleaming on the dressing-table. 'If he had time to pack all his clothes and all his papers, he'd have taken those things, too. Ever see a bald-headed man travel without a hairbrush?'

'And they're valuable, too? Do you think he rigged it himself?'

'Unlikely.'

'Then who?'

'I don't know – but we're going to find out. And as openers I think we'll pay a call on Gloriana downstairs.'

The kid in the sequin uniform was still at the doorway of the club. She said: 'Changed your mind, boys?'

'It's the gipsy in us,' Illya said.

They went through to a foyer that was a mixture of Tenth Avenue and the Taj Mahal. A cloakroom girl dressed in a grubby sari said: 'That will be one guinea each, gentlemen.'

'What for?' Illya asked.

'For the hats.'

'We never wear hats.'

'Too bad, ducks. It'll still cost you a guinea.'

They paid and pushed open swing doors emblazoned with scarlet dragons.

The big room beyond had the kind of lighting that is called discreet. It was fighting a losing battle against the swirling clouds of tobacco smoke. The only bright spot was the cone of light that picked out the three-piece combo of piano, guitar and bass. Half a dozen couples were moving like sleep-walkers on the pocket-size dance floor. The rest of the customers sat drinking at formica-topped tables, each with its own dim, scarlet-shaded lamp.

As Solo and Illya stood inside the door, letting their eyes get accustomed to the gloom, a man in a dinner-jacket came towards them. He was young, of middle height, with broad shoulders tapering to a thirty-two inch waist. His black, straight hair was glossy with Brylcreem, but his good looks were spoiled by a knife-scar that extended from right ear to chin. He looked like a Greek Cypriot.

'A table, gentlemen?' he asked.

Solo said: 'We'd like to talk to your boss.'

The professional smile stayed put but the brown eyes grew wary. 'Are you from the police?'

'No. Should we be?'

'I thought...' He let it tail away. 'I am afraid Madame is busy. May I ask why you wish to see her?'

Solo said definitely: 'You may not. Just tell her it's private. We won't keep her more than a few minutes.'

'Very well. If you will take a seat. A drink, perhaps, while you are waiting?'

'Scotch. On the rocks.'

'Certainly.' He went to the small bar that stood near the band dais, gave the order, then disappeared through a curtained doorway at the back of the room.

A girl wearing nylon fishnet tights and a bodice that ended almost where it began brought the drinks.

Illya asked: 'Compliments of the house?'

She said: 'Don't make me larf. It cracks me make-up. That'll be thirty bob.'

Illya stared glumly into the half-inch of liquid in his glass. 'I don't doubt that Madame is busy,' he said. 'She's probably arranging a take-over bid for Fort Knox.'

The man in the dinner jacket came back. He said: 'Madame will see you now. If you will come this way...'

They followed him through the curtained doorway and up three green-carpeted stairs to a door marked 'Private'. He knocked, turned the door handle and stood back for them to enter.

The room was more like a boudoir than an office. The walls were covered with expensive hand-blocked paper featuring pagodas, bamboos and small Chinese figures. The Chinese carpet was white and vividly flowered. There was a black lacquered table, heavily ornamented in gold, on which a slim vase held a single crimson rose. A black and gold cabinet, intricately carved, stood against the far wall. Sandalwood joss sticks smouldered before an ivory godling with a face of incarnate evil.

The woman went with the room. She sat facing the door in a chair that had a high back carved and coloured like a peacock's tail and quilted arms supported by grinning golden dragons. She wore a tunic and loose trousers in heavy white silk and there were white satin slippers on her tiny feet. No taller than a twelve-year-old girl, she looked like a frail Chinese doll.

Solo asked: '*You* are Madame Gloriana?'

She said: 'My name is Anna. Gloriana looks better on the facia, don't you think? Now what can I do for you gentlemen?'

'I am Napoleon Solo and this is my friend, Illya Kuryakin. We would like to ask you a few questions.'

'I shall try to answer them if they are not impertinent. You have not had trouble in my establishment, I hope.'

'Nothing like that,' Solo assured her. He took a picture of Price Hughes from his pocket and handed it to her. 'Have you ever seen this man?'

She smiled, showing white even teeth. 'Many times. He is my landlord. He owns this whole building.'

'That's interesting. When did you see him last?'

She frowned. 'I cannot remember exactly. About a year ago, I think. You must understand that there is no reason why we should meet. My business with him is transacted through his lawyers. I have seen him only by chance, as he went into or out of his offices next door.'

Illya said: 'You used the word "went" as if he had gone from there.'

She looked at him coldly. 'I did not mean to imply that. It is just that I believe he is frequently away from London for long periods. May I ask the reason for these questions?'

'We are trying to find him,' Solo said. 'He doesn't seem to be at home, and we have urgent business to discuss with him.'

'I am afraid I cannot help you. As I have explained, my contacts with Mr Hughes are not social.' She rose as gracefully as a Siamese cat and pressed a bell in the wall. The man in the dinner jacket appeared so quickly that he must have been waiting outside the door. She said: 'Dancer, the gentlemen are going. Please show them out.'

Dancer's expression said it would be a pleasure.

At the door Solo paused. He said: 'We are staying at

the Savoy, suite A25. If Mr Hughes turns up, perhaps you would get in touch with us.'

She smiled again. '*If* he turns up, I will ask him to contact you.'

When the door closed behind them she went immediately to the black and gold cabinet. She took out a telephone and dialled a number.

# CHAPTER NINE

THEY PICKED UP the Cortina and Solo drove through Trafalgar Square, down Whitehall and found a parking space in the shadow of the Houses of Parliament. Big Ben was striking ten-thirty as they crossed Bridge Street and walked down the stairs into the dive bar of an old-fashioned tavern.

Solo shouldered his way through the crowd at the counter, bought two Scotches and carried the drinks to a table where a man was sitting alone. He could have been any age from twenty-five to forty. His thin face was topped by mousy hair that needed cutting. He wore steel-rimmed spectacles with big round lenses and twists of grubby wool on the side-pieces near the ears. There was a glass of straight whisky on the table in front of him, and he was reading a late edition of the *Evening Standard*. Several other newspapers, rolled together, protruded from the pocket of his shabby raincoat.

Solo said: 'Hi! Solly.'

He looked up, surprised. 'Well, Napoleon! It's been a long time. So where have you sprung from?'

'Around and about,' Solo said, shaking his hand. 'This is my partner, Illya Kuryakin.'

The hand went out again. 'Nice to know you. What are you drinking?'

'You're too late,' Solo put the Scotch in front of him.

'What a friend,' Solly drained his own glass and raised the second. 'L'chayim!'

They drank.

Solo explained to Illya: 'Solly Gold is alleged to be chief crime reporter of the *Sunday Bugle*, but nobody ever saw him in the newsroom. He's on first-name terms with every copper and hoodlum in the West End and his capacity for hard liquor is illimitable.'

'The schmalz we can do without,' Solly said with dignity. 'You got something to ask? Ask.'

'All right. Give me a run-down on the cute little number who runs the Gloriana Club in Newport Street.'

'Anna?' He rubbed his hand slowly over his chin. 'What's to tell? She came out of nowhere a couple of years ago and opened up the way you see it now. Where she came from nobody knows. There's a story she got her money the hard way in Cardiff's "Tiger Bay", but that's what they say about any slant-eyed chippy who hits the scene. Me, I don't buy it. She's got too much class for a dockside grifter.'

'What do the police say?'

'Nothing. But nothing. Her record is clean. There was a rumour a while back about drug peddling in the club. The Yard investigated. There wasn't even the smell of a reefer.'

'Women?'

He spread his hands. 'Can you keep them out? Especially since the new Act. Where else have they got to go but the clubs? So women, naturally – but they've got to stay well-behaved. Any chatting up the customers and they're out on their fannies. They can sit at the bar. Any drinks you buy them, they get a percentage. You want to dance? O.K., they dance. But strictly no funny business on the premises.'

'You make it sound like a Sunday school,' Illya said. 'Do you know anything about a man called Price Hughes, too?'

'The nut-case next door? New Beginnings, and all that jazz?'

'That's the man.'

'Sure, I know him. So does everybody on the crime

beat. A do-gooder. Every time there's a hanging he organizes demonstrations outside the prison. In between, he saves souls. The way I hear it, there's a handout for every ex-con who climbs his stairs.' He considered. 'When he's there, that is. I haven't laid eyes on him in weeks.'

Solo bought three more drinks. When he returned, he asked: 'What about that floor-manager in the Gloriana, the hard boy who looks like a Greek?'

'You mean Dancer?' Solly said. 'He's a Malt and a three-time loser. First time for living on immoral earnings, the other two for grievous bodily harm. Funny thing, he's one of Hughes's protégés. When he came out after a chivving rap, the old man got him the job as Anna's bouncer.'

'That's funny. Anna said she never spoke to Price Hughes.'

'Go and argue with Anna,' Solly retorted. 'I'm telling it you the way I heard it.'

A barman came over and whispered something to him. He stood up. 'Telephone,' he explained. 'Don't go away.' He weaved slightly unsteadily towards the bar.

He was gone perhaps four minutes. When he came back his expression was less than benevolent. He said: 'Naturally, a coincidence. You wouldn't hold out on me, would you?'

Solo said: 'I might – if I knew what you were talking about. But I don't.'

'Questions, questions, questions – about Anna. About Dancer. About the old nut. But he don't know what I'm talking about.' Solly's gesture implored the ceiling to fall. Then his arms fell and he gripped the back of the chair. He leaned over, breathing whisky fumes into Solo's face.

'That was the office,' he snarled. 'A police patrol just found your old buddy Price Hughes on Hampstead Heath. Only it took them some time to recognize him. Somebody's been to work with a meat cleaver.'

'Well! Well!' Illya said mildly. 'And you thought we knew all along. Or maybe you think we killed him?'

'What I think or don't think, who cares?' Solly buttoned his raincoat with extreme care, pulling the frayed belt tight. 'What I know is that I've got a story to get – and that means getting the hell out to Hampstead right now. But don't think I won't be seeing you again.'

'Be our guest,' Solo invited. 'Want us to drive you to the Heath?'

'No. An office car is picking me up with a photographer.' The anger had gone out of his voice but there was still suspicion in his eyes. 'You don't want to tell me your end of it?'

Solo stood up and held out his hand. 'See us tomorrow, Solly, at the Savoy. We'll talk then.'

'Yes, and keep stumm, like always,' he grumbled. 'You cloak-and-dagger merchants, with you it's a one-way traffic.'

He shoved his hands into his pockets and swayed, with shoulders hunched, towards the exit.

Illya stared after him. 'Do you think he'll make it up the steps?'

'Don't let him fool you,' Solo said. 'He's as sober as the well-known judge. If there's anything to be found out at the Heath, Solly will find it. He's the best reporter in the business.'

'But will he tell us what he finds?'

'That,' said Solo, 'is one you can play on the nose.'

A cold wind was blowing across the river as they came up into Bridge Street, making them hurry to the shelter of the car. Illya turned the ignition key and the engine woke into life. 'Where now?'

'Back to the hotel. It's time we had words with New York.'

Illya turned the Cortina and drove up deserted Parliament Street, past the Cenotaph with its flags hanging in sculptured folds, and through Whitehall. Swinging left into Trafalgar Square, where students and tourists were still thronging around Nelson's column and the fountain, he asked suddenly: 'Well, who killed him?'

'Ask me why he was killed,' Solo said. 'That's easier. His death warrant was signed the moment you fouled up their Welsh operation. His cover was blown and his usefulness was finished. Thrush doesn't tolerate bunglers.'

'But why do the execution so publicly?' Illya objected. 'Thrush is usually more subtle.'

'There's that,' Solo agreed. 'A meat cleaver isn't exactly Machiavellian. It sounds more like one of the race gangs. It could be a kind of public warning, to encourage the others. But I've got other ideas.'

'Such as...?'

'It could be the body was planted for our benefit. You know: 'O.K., boys. The boss is dead. The game's up. So you can all go home.' Remember, we're still supposed to think Price Hughes was top man of the British Satrap. Morgan died before he could confess he blew the gaff.'

'It's possible.'

Illya swung the car into the forecourt of the Savoy Hotel and brought it to a halt outside the big doors. He said: 'You go on up and get through to Mr Waverly. I'll garage the car.'

Solo rode the elevator to the first floor, unlocked the door of suite A25 and put his finger on the light switch. A stunning jolt of electricity shot up his arm, momentarily paralysing him. In the same instant a bare, hairy forearm went round his neck in a Jap stranglehold. He countered quickly, trying to break the grip that threatened to squeeze the last gasp of air from his lungs. His foot went back, got a hold around the assailant's ankle. They went down in a heap, Solo on top.

The other man rolled, heaving Solo's body sideways. He wriggled free, smashing a murderous chop to Solo's adam's-apple as he rose. Solo grabbed wildly in the darkness, caught a handful of shirt and felt it tear. Then a kick crashed behind his ear.

When he came round, he was lying on a couch. There was a burning taste of liquor in his throat and whisky was dribbling down his chin. Illya, glass in hand, was standing over him.

He tried to sit up. Pain stabbed through his skull and he lay back again, closing his eyes against the glare of the ceiling chandelier. He asked feebly: 'What happened? Did the roof fall in?'

Illya said: 'They were waiting for you. Somebody had removed the switch cover. Really, Napoleon, I am surprised you fell for such an old trick.'

'It can happen to the best of us.' Solo raised himself slowly and cautiously opened one eye. He took the glass out of Illya's hand and drank. 'Did you see him.'

'No. I found you lying here. Our visitor had gone.'

Excuse me,' Solo went to the bathroom, ran cold water and sluiced it over his face. It felt good and he plunged his head in the bowl. He came back, towelling his hair. 'What was he after?'

'I think you interrupted him on a general exploratory mission,' Illya said. 'He has been through everything – cases, drawers, everything, and the place is a mess. But he also left something behind.'

He held out his hand. Solo saw in his palm a finely made gold medallion bearing the enamelled portrait of a woman saint. Attached to the loop was a broken length of platinum chain. Illya said: 'I found this on the floor by your head.'

Solo examined it. 'This is unusual, and it cost plenty,' he said. 'It's the kind of thing you usually see in Italy, Spain and the Latin-American countries. Mothers give them to their sons, and they're sometimes handed down from generation to generation as a sort of good-luck piece. I'd say this one is eighteenth-century. It shouldn't be too difficult to trace. Somebody among the Italian community in Soho ought to recognize it.'

'You are an optimist, my friend,' Illya said. 'Do you know how many Italians there are in Soho? And Spaniards and Cypriots and Maltese? And if someone recognized it, is it likely they would admit it? Our late visitor is a rough playmate.'

'I know it.' Solo massaged his aching head. 'But I also know these things have a strong superstitious value. And I think our little chum is going to move heaven and earth to get it back; so we have at least a starting point.'

He picked up the telephone, dialled Blodwen's number in Newport. When she answered, he asked: 'How soon can you make it to London?'

She said: 'Four hours. Maybe less, if I push it.'

'Fine. Then get going.'

'My God!' she said bitterly. 'Don't you think a girl needs any sleep?'

It was five in the morning when she knocked on the door of suite A25. Illya, in pyjamas and dressing-gown, let her in.

'All right,' she snapped. 'Where's the fire?'

He said: 'Don't ask me. This is Napoleon's party.'

'Where is he?'

'Sleeping, I hope. He's had a hard night.'

She spat out a rude Welsh word. 'You think spending the night dodging trucks on the motorway is a rest cure?' she demanded.

She dumped the poodle on the floor and peeled off her travelling coat. The poodle trotted happily around the room sniffing at the furniture, its stump tail wagging like a semaphore. Illya went to the telephone and called room service for coffee and toast.

Solo came from the bedroom. He was fully dressed, but his grooming was far from perfect. There was an ugly blue bruise from his swollen left ear to his cheekbone and his left eye was almost closed. He said: 'You made good time. Thanks for coming.'

'You're welcome.' She stared at his battered face. 'What hit you?'

He put a hand to his cheek. 'A boot, I think. Forgive my lack of a shave. The skin's a bit sensitive.'

'I can imagine. You should take something for it.'

A bell-boy arrived with the coffee, set the tray on a table convenient to the big couch, took his tip and went out quickly. The poodle trotted over to the table, sniffed, then got up on her hind legs and pirouetted like a ballet dancer, front paws outstretched.

'She can smell the toast,' Blodwen explained. 'That pooch has just one thought in the world. She's still too young for the other.'

Illya poured the coffee and handed a cup to Blodwen. She said: 'Thanks. Now, let's have the story.'

Solo outlined the events of the previous evening. She listened without interruption. When he had finished she picked up the medallion and looked at both sides. Without raising her eyes, she asked: 'What do you want me to do?'

He smiled. 'Have you ever worked as a dancehall hostess.'

'Me? Not on your celebrated nellie.'

'Well, here's your chance to broaden your experience,' Solo said. 'I want you to get yourself a job at the Gloriana. That shouldn't be difficult. Keep your eyes and ears open for any odd scraps of information – but above all, wear the medallion in plain sight. Never show yourself without it.'

'You think Anna is at the bottom of the nonsense?'

'I don't know,' he replied. 'But she's involved somewhere along the line. I want to know just how deeply.'

'Check! And where do I live?'

'Get yourself a room in Soho – Greek Street, Wardour Street, somewhere like that. Not too expensive, but not too cheap, either. The kind of place any hardworking tramp would choose.'

'That's what I love about you,' Blodwen said, 'You always pick the graceful phrase.'

She stood up. 'Now, if you boys will excuse me, I'll borrow the bedroom for an hour. I'm dead on my feet. Wake me at nine and I'll start house-hunting.'

# CHAPTER TEN

SOLLY GOLD arrived at noon. There were dark shadows beneath his eyes and his normally pale face looked almost deathly. A badly-rolled cigarette drooped from a corner of his mouth.

He took the whisky Solo gave him, drained it at a gulp and held out the glass for a refill. He said: 'At my time of life I've got to be up all night chasing stiffs. I should have my brains examined. You seen the dailies?'

Illya said: 'We've read them. They don't say much.'

'So what's to say? They got a body. They got a name for the body. The Yard are making inquiries. What else? You think the police are telling what they know?' He puffed futilely on the dead cigarette, took it out of his mouth, looked at it distastefully and tossed it into the fireplace.

'There's no doubt it was Price Hughes?' Solo asked.

'Not a chance. The face his own mother wouldn't recognize. Whoever carved him took a real pleasure in it. And there were no papers in his pockets. But the prints were positive.'

'Fingerprints?' Illya repeated.

'Yeah, prints. It seems he wasn't always a do-gooder. Criminal Records had a full set of his dabs from "way back". For what, don't ask. Even *me* they're not telling.' He sounded genuinely indignant.

'According to the *Express* the police have got a lead,' Illya said.

'Oh! sure. Like always. You think they're going to

admit they're up a gum tree? No weapon? No suspect? No motive? But one thing they have got. The old man was plenty dead when he was dumped on the Heath.'

'You mean he was killed elsewhere?'

'A long ways elsewhere is my guess. And what's more, he was frozen practically stiff – like he'd been in a refrigerator a couple of days.'

Solly accepted a third Scotch, eyeing Solo's bruises with professional interest. 'Now,' he said, 'suppose you trade a little information. Like, for instance, how you get the shiner.'

'All right – but it's strictly off the record. When the time's right you'll get it exclusive. Fair?'

'Fair,' Solly confirmed. 'Till you say so, I'm an oyster.'

Solo told him the story.

He rolled another cigarette from coarse pipe tobacco and licked the paper thoughtfully. He had to relight the end three times before it would burn properly. At last he said: 'If you're fingering Dancer for the murder you can think again. He'd kill his own brother for sixpence and sleep easy. But it's a matter of technique. Dancer's strictly a chiv man. With a knife he's an artist. And with him it's a business. Nothing personal, you understand. But this Hughes job – what a butchery! And the boy who did it had himself a ball.' He considered. 'Maybe you remember, there was a mob in Brooklyn that worked with Murder, Inc. They used choppers. It was that kind of job. Crude.'

He went through the ritual of buttoning his raincoat to the chin, though the sun was hot on the windows of the room. 'Got to go. Thanks for the drinks... and the lowdown. Anything I hear that we can't print, I'll keep you posted.'

'Now what do you make of that?' Illya asked when the door had closed behind the reporter.

'You tell me. It's a mess. But some part of the answer's in the Gloriana. Dancer may not have been the killer, but five will get you ten it was his boot I felt last night. The raid, coming on top of our visit to Anna, was too coincidental. And who else knew exactly where to find us?'

'It could have been an ordinary prowler.'

'Prowlers don't fool with the electrical fittings,' Solo pointed out. 'They get in, turn the place over, and get out fast. Our man seems to have been looking for information, not for loot.'

'That makes sense. But what else have we got?'

Solo said: 'The big tie-in is that Price Hughes owned the building, ran his business and lived – at least, for some of the time – next door to the Gloriana. If Solly is to be believed, and his information is usually twenty-carat, we also know that Anna was lying when she claimed she had no personal dealings with the old man. According to Solly, she gave Dancer his job because Hughes asked her to do it. Why lie about it? There's also the story that she came from Cardiff to London. That may mean a lot or nothing at all, but the Welsh background is certainly interesting.

'On the other hand, she has no police record and the club is in the clear. We know her floor manager is a thug, but again the story is that he's keeping his nose clean.'

Illya nodded. 'And that's it. There's not a shred of evidence to connect the club or anyone in it with the killing. Or, for that matter, with the attack on you last night. It seems to me that our one solid lead is the medallion.'

'That's what I'm banking on,' Solo said. 'I think Dancer will make a move when Blodwen shows up with it round her neck. Meanwhile we'll start checking on Anna's daily round.'

The telephone rang. He picked up the receiver. Blodwen's voice came cheerfully over the wire. She said: 'I've got a flat in Berwick Street. You'll like it. It's got G-Plan furniture, plumbing straight from the Ark and mice behind the skirtings. The rent book says seven pounds a week but I had to pay the landlord twenty – and six months in advance. Ain't life wonderful for us working girls?'

'My heart bleeds for you,' Solo said. 'Want us to come over?'

'Yes, do that. In this house a gal's nobody without gentlemen callers. In fact, we put postcard ads in a neighbourhood store to encourage them.'

'You're learning fast. We'd better get over there before the replies start coming in.'

A taxi dropped them in Brewer Street and they walked the rest of the way, shouldering through the bargain-hunters crowding the stalls in Berwick Street's open market, where you can buy anything from a rusty flintlock to a string of Spanish onions. The number Blodwen had given Solo turned out to be narrow doorway sandwiched between two shops. A woman was leaning against the doorpost, smoking a Gauloise cigarette. She wore a peasant-type silk blouse that strained against massive breasts, a tight black skirt, and patent-leather shoes with heels that were more like six-inch nails. She had coarse black hair piled high and grey eyes that had seen everything.

She switched on a smile that was meant to be inviting. 'You boys looking for something?'

'Just visiting,' Solo said. 'A friend moved in here today.'

'Oh! her.' She lost interest. 'She's up on the second floor. If she's in.'

The staircase, covered with ancient grey carpet, was steep and ricketty. It had a sad indefinable smell compounded of cheap scent, damp and grime. The once white walls bore marks of the passing of many bodies.

On the door facing the head of the second flight a cheap printed visiting card was secured with the a thumbtack. It read: 'Miss Yvonne Grey. Modelling.'

Solo pressed the yellowing bell-push and a two-tone chime sounded through the wood.

The girl who opened the door wore a black nylon

jumper, skin-tight scarlet jeans and black stiletto-heel shoes. Her hair was tightly curled and bright henna red. Lashes thick with mascara fringed eyes of startling china-blue.

She smiled widely and said: 'Surprise! Surprise!'

'My God!' Solo said. 'What have you been doing to yourself?'

She put a finger to lips the colour of over-ripe tomatoes. 'Can't talk on the doorstep. Let's go in.'

She led the way into a pocket-size sitting-room that was overcrowded with shabby pseudo-Scandinavian furniture. The poodle cocked a beady eye from its basket near the gas fire, yapped briefly and subsided.

'A drink?' Blodwen asked.

'No, thanks. You still haven't explained the fancy dress.'

'Protective colouring,' she said. 'If I'm going to join the soiled doves in the Gloriana, I've to look the part.' She struck a Mae West pose and patted the incendiary curls. 'Don't you like it?'

Illya said: 'Your eyes. What happened to your eyes?'

'Contact lenses. No gal should be without them.' Then more seriously she said: 'There's always the chance that somebody might show up who saw me in Corwen or Newport. I had to do a complete remodelling job.'

'That makes sense,' Solo agreed. 'Have you been around to see Anna?'

'No need. She doesn't employ regular hostesses. Any girl who's free, white and twenty-one can put in an evening's stint as decoration at the bar – provided she's properly introduced. And that's been taken care of.' She grinned. 'I expect you met my chaperone downstairs.'

'The lass with the armour-piercers?'

'The same. She has the flat below. She's one of those hard-boiled hustlers with a heart of gold, and she's taken me under her wing. I do my first stint at the Gloriana to-night.'

'Well, watch it,' Solo warned. 'There are limits to what Alexander Waverly expects in the line of duty.'

'Don't worry. I'm a long-time student of Dear Abby.'

There came a faint morse-like tapping. Blodwen said: 'Oh – oh!' and went to the door.

The woman in the peasant blouse came in. She looked from Solo to Illya, then back to Blodwen. She asked: 'Everything O.K., dear?' Her low-pitched voice had a Continental intonation.

Blodwen said: 'Everything's fine, Merle. These are two old friends of mine. They just dropped in to see I was settled proper.'

'That's O.K., then.' She switched on the smile. 'Pleased to meet you.'

Blodwen went to a glass-fronted cabinet, got out a bottle and poured four large gins.

'Ta, dear.' Merle raised her glass in a gesture that embraced them all. 'Cheers!'

They drank.

Merle said: 'Excuse me dropping in, dear. I was a bit worried. I thought they might be fuzz.'

'The Law?' Blodwen said. 'These boys? That's a laugh.'

'I'm glad.' She didn't ask any questions.

Illya said politely: 'This is a nice place you have here.'

She looked around. 'Not bad – but the overheads are killing.' Then to Blodwen: 'You better be getting ready, dear. I thought we'd have a bite together before we go on to the club. I shake up a good ravioli – out of a can.'

Blodwen poured her another gin. 'Give me a couple of minutes. Talk to these lads while I'm putting on my face.' She disappeared into the bedroom, the poodle at her heels.

Merle looked after her. She said: 'She's a nice kid. You known her long?'

'Quite a while,' Illya said. 'We have a mutual uncle.'

'That's nice. I didn't realize you was relatives or I wouldn't have butted in.'

'We're glad you did,' Solo assured her. 'She can use a friend.'

'Yes, she don't seem to know nobody in the Smoke – you excepting, of course.'

'If it isn't a rude question, how did you come to meet her?' Illya asked.

'I was having an eye-opener in a pub by the Windmill Theatre and she drifted in. She didn't seem to have no place to go, so I fixed her up. A girl can get into bad company if she ain't careful. And like I said, she's a nice kid.' Her mouth twisted bitterly. 'Too good for them bleeding Maltese to get their hooks in her.'

'She'll be all right with you, though.' Solo said.

'Sure. I'm an independent operator, you see. I don't have no truck with the rings.'

Blodwen returned. She had exchanged the slacks and sweater for a green sack dress that ended four inches above her knees. The medallion swung at waist level from a long rolled-gold chain.

Merle eyed it, puzzled and astonished. She said: 'Look, kid, you can't wear that thing in the Gloriana. Not if you don't want trouble.'

'Why not?' Blodwen demanded. 'It's pretty.'

'Pretty or not, you can't wear it. I'm not asking where you got it. That's not my business. All I know is, the last time I seen it was round the neck of French Louise, and if she catches you with it there'll be bloody murder. So be a sensible kid and take it off.'

'Why should I? I came by it honestly. And if somebody wants to start something, I can take care of myself.'

Merle shrugged. 'O.K., dear. Please yourself. It's your funeral. But don't say I didn't warn you. French Louise is a bitch in spades.'

She stood up. 'Let's be on our way. Nice to meet you boys.'

Blodwen settled the poodle in its basket with a dish of meat, then she pulled on a black nylon fur coat and ushered them to the door. They walked down to the first floor together. The girls stopped there, and Blodwen said: 'Thanks for coming. Now you know where we live, drop round again.'

The market had closed down and Berwick Street was practically empty. Solo and Illya walked through to Brewer Street and caught a cab to the hotel.

As the taxi threaded through the first rush of theatre traffic Illya asked: 'What's now?'

Solo said: 'The trap's baited. All we can do is wait. I've got a feeling it won't be long.'

When they got up to the suite Solo went into the bedroom and pulled out a suitcase. He unlocked it, took out a black transmitter, and placed it on the bed. He unwound aerial wire, draping it carefully in loops around the walls. Then he tuned in and said: 'Open channel D.'

The voice of the operator in the brownstone block near the East River was distorted by static. She said: 'This is a lousy line. Sunspots or something. Why didn't you bounce your call off Early Bird?'

'We'll have to get U.N.C.L.E. to put up his own satellite,' Solo said. 'Put me on to I.D., please.'

There was a second's delay and then a male voice announced: 'Identifications and Records.'

'Hi! Al,' Solo greeted. 'I want all you can get me on a woman called Anna, surname unknown. She runs a club called Gloriana in Newport Street, London. She is Oriental, probably Chinese but could be Indonesian, about thirty years old, height not more than five feet, weight around ninety-eight pounds, no visible distinguishing marks. Antecedents unknown, but rumoured to have come to London from Cardiff. No criminal record, as far as I can trace.'

'You say the sweetest things.' Al sounded bitter. 'All of a sudden I'm a magician? Why don't you try Scotland Yard? The West End squad must know her, even if she's clean.'

'I don't want to bring the Yard into it at this stage.'

'O.K., I'll do what I can. When do you want the dope?'

Solo said: 'Yesterday,' and tuned out hurriedly.

He unshipped the aerial, packed the set back in the suitcase and went into the living-room. He told Illya: 'Ring room service and ask them to send dinner up here. I'll call Al back in a couple of hours and see if he's managed to produce.'

'Anna?'

'Who else?'

It was ten-thirty when the phone rang.

Solo put down the paperback he was reading and picked up the receiver.

Blodwen's voice said chirpily: 'Napoleon? Can you do me a teeny-weeny little favour?'

'Where are you?'

'I'm in Bow Street police station. Be a darling and come and bail me out.'

# CHAPTER ELEVEN

THE DESK SERGEANT was a middle-aged man with a deeply-tanned face that looked like old leather. There was a Burma Star in the row of ribbons above the pocket of his tunic. He said: 'Yvonne Grey. I don't know why she had to drag you out of bed. She could have bailed herself out if she'd wanted to. We weren't anxious to keep her.'

'I suppose she had her reasons,' Solo said. 'What is she booked for?'

'Disorderly conduct. She was having a bit of a fight with another woman in Newport Street. We picked them both up.'

'Where is she now?'

'In the cells. Sleeping it off, I hope.' He signalled to a young constable. 'Bring Mitchell up.'

He opened a drawer and took out an orange form. 'You sign this. Better read it first. If she fails to surrender to her bail it'll cost you ten quid.'

'She'll show up.' Solo signed along the dotted line.

The young policeman reappeared with Blodwen beside him. Her red curls were tousled, the front of her dress was torn, and there was an angry furrow where fingernails had ripped down her cheek, but she seemed in high spirits.

She said: 'Thanks for coming to the rescue. Have you completed the formalities?'

The sergeant put her handbag on the counter and gave her a form. 'Check the contents and sign for them,' he told her. 'And remember, you've got to be back here at the court at ten sharp tomorrow.'

'On the dot,' she promised. 'And thanks for your hospitality.'

They went out into the street. Solo hailed a taxi and gave the cabbie the Berwick Street address.

'Now,' he said, when they were back in Blodwen's flat, 'perhaps you'll explain what you've been up to.'

She went to the cabinet and poured drinks. 'We're making progress,' she said. 'You were right about the medallion. It was a sensation. That's how I ended up in chokey.'

She handed Solo his glass, took her own and settled herself comfortably on the settee with the poodle in her lap.

'We got to the Gloriana around eight o'clock,' she began. 'The place was half-empty then. Just a couple of girls at the bar and a few customers at the tables. Dancer drifted over after a while and had a few words with Merle. If he recognized the medallion he didn't show it. He had a quick drink and then got on with his job. Apart from saying good-evening he didn't give me a tumble. Like I told you, the girls drift in and out and no questions asked.

'Anna only showed up once. She came into the room, looked around to see that everything was going smoothly and then went away again, presumably back to her office.

'The fun didn't start until half-past nine. That's when French Louise arrived. She was obviously as high as a kite, and once she got her beady eyes on the medallion she was fit to be tied. I'll skip the details, but her main complaint seemed to be that I had pinched her boy friend, a character called Scalesi. She kept pushing his photograph under my nose and yelling at me in gutter French. And all the time she kept trying to grab the medallion.

'Merle tried to calm her down but it was like trying to plug a volcano with a medicine cork. In the end Dancer gave us both the old heave-ho out on to the cold hard sidewalk, and it was there the battle started. The boys in blue broke it up and the next thing you know, we're in the Black Maria and on the way to Bow Street.'

She finished her drink and went to the cabinet for another. 'I sent for you,' she explained, 'because I hoped you'd be in time to get a look at French Louise before they took us down to the cells. But that sergeant was too efficient. Now you'll have to wait until the morning when we come up before the beak.' She raised her glass. 'Here's to crime!'

'You've done a good job,' Solo said. He stood up. 'Now I'd better get out of here before I ruin your reputation.'

'You must be joking,' she retorted. 'In this house you'd do it more good if you stayed all night.'

He shook his head sadly. 'You're showing a dedication to your work,' he said, 'that is beginning to disturb me.'

'That's what Stanislavsky does for a gal. It's the Method.'

'Well, don't get carried away. I'll see you in court in the morning.'

Illya was waiting up in the hotel suite. He said: 'New York came through with a message from I.D. They've checked on Anna. Her description ties up with an enterprising young woman called Anna Soo Lee, born 1934 in Shanghai. Soo Lee's father was a minor war lord. He joined up with Chiang Kai-shek and went to Formosa in 1949. For some reason Anna didn't go with him. She showed up briefly as a dancer in Singapore and in Sydney, Australia, and was next reported as the girl friend of a polo-playing maharajah, complete with white Mercedes and all the trimmings. Something broke that up, but she came out of it with quite a stake. She arrived in Britain by air in 1960 and for some reason only known to herself settled down in Bute Town, Cardiff – the old "Tiger Bay". For the record, incidentally, Bute Town these days is as respectable as Poughkeepsie and a model of racial integration. The rough stuff went out with hobble skirts.'

'That sounds like our Anna,' Solo said. 'How many times has she blotted her copybook?'

Illya frowned. 'Never. That's the strange thing. You could say her career has been colourful but circumspect. She's never been within shouting distance of trouble officially. Yet somewhere along the line she has managed to get together a very considerable fortune – which is at least unusual for Shanghai dance-hall girls.'

'Maybe the maharajah was generous.'

'Maybe. And there's also a story that he was one of the principals in an international gold smuggling ring operating out of Bombay. But like everything else connected with Anna Soo Lee, it's unproven.'

'Interesting but unhelpful,' Solo commented. 'Well, I'm going to bed. Tomorrow looks like being a tough day.'

Business was brisk at the morning session of Bow Street magistrates court. Too-liberal celebrants of victory and defeat in an international football match at Wembley Stadium had swelled the crime-sheet. One by one, with blinding hangovers, they filed into the dock to listen dully to the recital of their errors on the night before. They were followed by the normal procession of ladies of the town who had bucked the provisions of the Street Offences Act. Then Blodwen and French Louise were put up together.

French Louise was a battered synthetic blonde with the elfin charm of a Sherman tank. She stood five feet two, weighed 140 pounds, and most of the avoirdupois was distributed around her chest and hips. The fingers that gripped the edge of the dock were short and thick, with bitten nails.

She listened sullenly while the young constable gave evidence of the battle on the Newport Street pavement. It was his first major arrest and he made quite a production of the story. He left no doubt in the minds of the court that French Louise had been the challenger.

'Anything known?' the magistrate asked.

Louise, it transpired, had a string of convictions for soliciting, shoplifting and disturbing the public peace ranging back to the days of Pearl Harbour.

'Have you anything to say for yourselves?'

They kept silent. The bench considered sentence.

Blodwen, as a first offender, escaped with a nominal fine. Louise was not so lucky. She got the maximum.

The size of the fine made her gasp. 'You got to be joking,' she said. 'Where the hell would I find that kind of money?'

Blodwen cut in quickly: 'I'll pay it, your worship.'

He nodded. 'Very well.'

The usher called the next case.

'You didn't have to do that,' Louise said grudgingly as they walked to the office to pay the fines. 'I wasn't asking no favours from you.'

'Forget it,' Blodwen said. 'Why should you go inside for nothing? Honest to God, I never even met your boy friend. Let's get the hell out of here and have a drink.'

'O.K., then. If you've still got the price.'

'Don't worry. My friend is in the pub down the street. He'll pay.'

Solo was sitting in the panelled saloon bar of the old Coach and Horses in Bow Street. He clucked sympathetically and told Louise: 'They really threw the book at you.'

'Yeah, the bleeders. Still, I suppose I asked for it.'

Solo gave her a large gin and it went down in one gulp. He gave her another, and she said: 'Thanks. That hits the spot.'

There was still suspicion in her eyes, despite her forced friendliness. She said to Blodwen: 'I'm not starting anything but I still want to know. If Scalesi didn't give you my luck-piece, where did you get hold of it?'

'I gave it to her.' Solo replied.

'And how did you come by it?' she demanded.

'I picked it up some place,' he said vaguely. 'The question is, how do we know it was yours in the first place?'

'Ask any of the girls. They've all seen me wearing it. Till it got pinched, that is.'

'Mind telling us where you got it?'

'That's my business. And why are you so goddam interested, anyway.'

Solo took four £5 notes from his pocket and laid them on the bar. 'I'm just naturally curious,' he said, 'and I always pay for my whims.'

'Well, it's no secret.' She picked up the notes and put them in her shabby handbag. 'I got it from the holy Joe in Newport Street. You know, the old geezer who runs the New Beginnings lark.'

'Was he trying to reform you?'

She laughed shortly. 'In bed?'

Blodwen asked: 'But what made you think your friend gave it to me?'

'Scalesi? He's no friend of mine. Not any more,' she said bitterly. 'He beat the hell out of me and went off with everything he could lay his filthy paws on. The luck-piece was part of it.'

'He sounds charming,' Solo said. 'When did this happen?'

'A couple of months ago. I've never laid eyes on him since.'

'What does he look like?'

She opened her handbag, sorted through a conglomeration of letters, lipstick, compact, comb and other feminine junk and came up with a cracked, grubby snapshot. It had been taken on Brighton Pier and it showed a flashily good-looking young thug dressed in leather jacket and skin-tight jeans.

She said: 'That's him. Keep it if you want to. Gawd knows he gave me plenty to remember him by – to my dying day.'

Solo put the picture in his wallet. He put a pound note on the bar and said: 'Have one for the road. Sorry we have to rush away.'

She said indifferently: 'Be seeing you around,' and rapped on the counter for service.

Merle was at her post in the doorway when they returned to the house in Berwick Street. She looked relieved when she saw Blodwen step from the taxi.

'I've been worrying myself sick,' she greeted her. 'I thought they must've put you away. I warned you not to tangle with Louise, didn't I? She's murder, that bitch.'

'It wasn't too bad,' Blodwen said. 'Cost me two quid. Come up to the flat. We want to talk to you.'

She left Solo and Merle together in the sitting-room and went into the kitchen to brew coffee.

Solo asked: 'What do you know about a man called Scalesi?'

'I've heard Louise talk about him. She was living with him,' Merle said. 'I never saw him, though.'

He showed her the snapshot, and she said: 'You know the nicest people. That's not Scalesi. It's a lousy young tearaway called Pietro Bambini. You want my advice, you'll steer clear of him. He's a mad dog.'

'You mean he's insane?'

'I mean he's crazy. He beats people up for the fun of it. He likes to see blood. Real professionals won't work with him. He scares them stiff. They know one day he'll do a "topping" job – you know, murder – and they don't want to be around when it happens.'

Blodwen came in with the coffee. She asked: 'Where does this charmer hang out? We'd like to meet him.'

'Meet him?' she repeated. 'Are you out of your mind? Didn't Louise tell you what he done to her?'

She grew suddenly cautious. 'Look, who are you two, anyhow? I don't like all these questions, and I thought there was something screwy about you from the first. What are you up to?'

Solo said: 'We're not police, if that's what is worrying

you. We represent an international organization known as U.N.C.L.E. with headquarters in New York.' He showed her his identification card. 'You can do a big service to your country and to the world if you will help us.'

'You could've come clean in the first place,' she grumbled. 'I've read about U.N.C.L.E. in one of the magazines. Some kind of secret service, isn't it?'

'Near enough,' Solo admitted.

'Yeah. Well, just because I'm in my business don't mean I'm not a good citizen. I pay my rates and taxes, don't I? What do you want from me?'

'Tell us about Bambini.'

'Him I don't want no part of,' she said emphatically. 'He's poison, and I still say keep away. If he thought I'd grassed on him, he'd cut my heart out.'

'We'll see you're protected,' Blodwen promised. 'Just tell us where we can find him.'

'Who knows,' she said. 'He's in and out of the Gloriana most evenings, though I haven't seen him lately. He drives a car for that Chinese dame who owns the place.'

'Anna?'

'Yes, that's her. It's a big black job, very classy. She keeps it in a mews garage off Tottenham Court Road. Bambini lives in a room over the top.' She gave them the address.

Solo said: 'Thank you. Now, just one more thing. Did you ever go into the kitchens at the Gloriana?'

She looked surprised. 'Yes, once or twice. Why?'

'Have they got a refrigerator there?'

'They've got a cold store room,' she said, 'big enough to hold an ox.'

'I thought they might have,' he nodded. 'Things are beginning to add up nicely.'

# CHAPTER TWELVE

THE MEWS was off Stephen Street, not far from the junction of Oxford Street and Tottenham Court Road. It was a cul-de-sac about one hundred and fifty yards long which at one time had housed the carriages of noble families. Now the stables had been converted into lock-up garages with flats above.

Illya drove to the far end of the mews, made a U-turn and parked with the bonnet of the Cortina facing into Stephen Street. He remained sitting behind the wheel while Solo got out and walked back, looking for the number Merle had given him. He found it half-way down the right-hand side: a pair of green-painted garage doors with a smaller door beside them.

He pressed the bell-push on the small door and waited. There was no response. He took out a bunch of keys and tried the lock on the garage doors. At the third attempt the wards clicked. He swung the doors wide enough to admit his body, then pulled them shut behind him.

Enough daylight filtered through the grimy windows for him to see that the car was a black Humber Hawk. The front bumper was decorated with a row of motoring club badges, but on the near side there was a gap that showed up like a broken tooth. Examining the bracket in the light of his pocket torch Solo could see that the missing badge had been torn violently from its place.

The leather upholstery of the seats was clean. There was nothing but a road map and a spare lamp bulb in the glove compartment on the dashboard. The pockets in the car doors were empty.

Solo went to the back of the car and unlocked the boot. The torch beam illuminated a crumpled length of burlap and a wheel jack. There were dark stains on the burlap that could have been oil or blood.

Solo took out his pocket-knife, cut a small piece from the stained material and tucked it into an envelope. He closed the boot quietly, then went out and let the doors click shut.

'Any luck?' Illya asked as the Cortina moved out into Stephen Street.

'I don't know,' Solo said, 'but I think it's time we had words with Solly Gold.'

The hands of the clock over the Law Courts were pointing to half-past seven when they went into the Wig and Pen Club in the Strand.

The Wig and Pen is housed in the only building in the Strand that can claim to have survived both the Fire of London in 1666 and the Fire Blitz in 1940–41. There is no elevator to the penthouse restaurant because the 300-year-old staircase, the only one of its kind, is protected under the Ancient Monuments Act. Despite the recent invasion of expense-account types from advertising and public relations the club retains much of its original character as a rendezvous for barristers and top newspapermen.

Except for Monty, the barman, the Front Page bar's only occupant was Solly Gold. He was sitting on a high stool at the far end of the counter, nursing a whisky straight. He looked undressed without his raincoat.

He said: 'So what brings you to the fabled Street of Adventure – and bushwah? Have a drink.'

'Don't ever let the boys on the *Bugle* hear you said that,' Solo advised. 'What do you know about a hoodlum called Pietro Bambini?'

'Enough,' Solly said. 'Born in Greek Street, Soho, father unknown. His mother was an Italian waitress –

part of the time. Educated, approved schools and Borstal. Ran with the Focacci mob until the Carey brothers chased Focacci out of the West End and took over. Now he's a freelance, hiring out for the really dirty work. He'd cut his own mother up for kicks. He's a nutter. And vicious with it.'

'That's the way I hear it. Did you know he drives for Anna?'

'No. That's new. I'd say she was taking a chance. Like I say, he's no tame bunny. You're sure of your facts?'

'Pretty sure.'

'Funny. I'd have thought she was smarter. Now why would she want to bother with a schlemiel like Bambini?'

'That,' said Solo, 'is the jackpot question.'

He outlined the events of the night and day, keeping only Merle's name out of the story. When he told of his visit to the garage in the mews, Solly's eyes suddenly gleamed behind the steel-rimmed spectacles.

He asked: 'You're positive one of the badges had been smashed off the bracket? It couldn't have been cut off or rusted off?'

'Positive. The break was jagged and the metal was twisted as if somebody had hit it with a sledgehammer.'

Solly said: 'It's time you brought the Yard in on this. The night Hughes' body was found on Hampstead Heath a hit-and-run driver killed a motor-cyclist on the Spaniards Road near Jack Straw's Castle.'

Solo explained to Illya: 'That's the road that runs along the top of the Heath just north of the Vale of Health. It's on a direct route to the centre of London.'

'Check,' said Solly, 'And guess what they found by the smashed bike.'

'I'm ahead of you,' Solo said. 'And they'd have it at the Yard?'

'Believe me, they're treasuring it. And that bit of sacking you clipped – the lab boys would like to see that, too.'

'Fine. Whom do I call?'

Solly drained his glass and stood up. 'Leave it to me. It'll be a pleasure.'

He retrieved his raincoat from Ted, the porter, and hurried off to the cab rank in the shadow of St Clement Danes.

Solo and Illya strolled leisurely along the Strand to the hotel. They found Blodwen waiting in the suite. She had washed the henna out of her hair and removed the blue-irised contact lenses. She had switched to a lightweight tweed and had exchanged the stiletto-heeled patent leathers for London-tan walking shoes. Dolly, the poodle, was freshly shampooed and curled and sported a brand-new collar.

'There's no point in keeping the flat on now that Merle knows who I am, and those contact lenses hurt like hell,' Blodwen explained. 'I've checked in on the floor below, where I'll be handy if you need me. Right now I propose to catch dinner and have an early night.'

'We'll join you,' Illya said. 'For dinner, of course.'

They had reached the coffee stage when Solly Gold approached their table with a companion.

'I phoned your number and the switchboard told me where to find you,' he said. 'This is Detective-Inspector Jevons, of the C.I.D.'

Jevons looked nothing like the sleuths of popular fiction. He had close-cropped iron-grey hair, blue eyes set rather too close to an over-large nose, prominent ears and a hard square jaw. He wore a navy-blue, double-breasted suit, a white shirt and collar with a dark grey tie, and black shoes with rounded toecaps.

He sat down, accepted a coffee, and proceeded to load a brier with dark flake tobacco.

He said: 'Thanks for the tip, Mr Solo. I've heard about you, though, of course, you U.N.C.L.E. chaps normally work with the Special Branch. I don't know what job you're on now, and I'm asking no questions. That's S.B. business. If you want our assistance, you know you'll get it. But hit-and-run driving is definitely in my province, especially when there's a suspicion of cold-blooded murder.'

'You think Bambini killed Price Hughes?'

'I think nothing, Mr Solo. I go on evidence. A great deal is going to depend on what we find in the garage. We do know that the stain on the material you sent to us by Mr Gold has been confirmed to be human blood, but the fact that you found it in the boot of a car known to have been driven by Bambini is no proof that he had anything to do with it.'

He pushed his chair back and stood up. 'And now, if the young lady will excuse us, we could make a move.'

Blodwen said: 'Don't wait for the bill. I'll see to it. If you happen to need me I'll be back at the hotel.'

Solly Gold looked pessimistically at the inspector. 'I suppose there's no chance I'll be invited along for the ride?'

'You know better than that, Mr Gold.'

'Yes, I know. It's the story of my life.'

Illya, Solo and the inspector left the restaurant together. A police car dropped them in Stephen Street and they completed the journey on foot.

A man in a shabby suit and cloth cap emerged from the shadow at the entrance to the mews. Jevons asked him: 'Anything moving?'

'All quiet,' he replied. 'The car's in the garage and the place above is in darkness. Nobody's been near it.'

'Thank you, Sergeant. Keep your eyes skinned.'

'Yes, Sir.'

The lock on the garage door turned easily to Solo's key. The three men entered and Solo switched on his torch. The beam danced over the Humber's bonnet and came to rest on the bumper.

The inspector crouched and examined the gap in the row of badges. He ran a finger over the short tongue of metal on the twisted bracket. Then he took another badge from his pocket and tried it against the fracture. The irregular edges of badge and tongue fitted exactly.

'That clinches it,' Jevons said. 'This was the car that killed the motor-cyclist. This badge was found only a few feet from the body.' He straightened and pointed to the near wing. 'Somebody's been doing some respraying, too, and the job's been done in a hurry.'

They shut the garage and went back to the plain clothes man on the corner. Jevons told him: 'If Bambini shows up, grab him and bring him in. I want him for questioning in connection with the hit-and-run on Hampstead Heath. Have you got assistance?'

'Yes, sir. Two constables.' He indicated where they were posted in the darkness.

'Good. Well, don't take chances. You know Bambini. He's sure to be carrying a knife. But get him, Sergeant. I want him badly.'

'He won't get away,' the sergeant promised.

The police car snaked through the thick traffic in Tottenham Court Road, heading back to New Scotland Yard. Jevons, sitting beside the driver, spoke into the radio-telephone. Solo gathered that he was talking to his superintendent at headquarters.

The car cut down Northumberland Avenue and on to the Embankment, where the lights of the South Bank were reflected in dancing patterns on the black waters of the Thames. It turned in through the big gates within a stone's throw of Westminster Bridge and the driver drew it smoothly to a halt.

The inspector led the way to his office on the second floor of the Yard building. It was a cubby-hole of a room, painted in a depressing shade of green. It contained a battery of green steel filing cabinets, several straight-backed chairs and a brown, government-issue table that held three telephones. The only wall decorations were an electric clock and a calendar which showed an improbable English village.

Jevons indicated a couple of chairs. He said: 'Make yourselves comfortable – if you can. I'll have to leave you for a couple of minutes while I have a word with my chief. Smoke, if you want to.'

He returned five minutes later. Behind him came a uniformed policeman carrying a metal tray with three thick mugs of canteen tea.

Jevons said: 'I'm sorry we can't manage anything stronger. The wheels of crime are lubricated with this stuff. We drink gallons of it, day and night.'

Illya tasted it. It was scalding hot and had a flavour reminiscent of tanning solution. He said: 'It's excellent,' and put the mug carefully on the floor beside his chair.

'An all-station call has gone out for Bambini,' the inspector said. 'By this time there are C.I.D. men and uniformed patrols combing every dive and gaff in the West End. If he's in London we'll find him. It may take a bit longer if he's got out of town, but we'll get him in the end. Now, all we can do is wait.'

'You've tried the Gloriana, of course?' Solo asked.

'First port of call,' Jevons assured him. 'Not a sign of him. But we've got one man inside the building and two men in Newport Street, covering the place in case he shows up.'

'Have your people talked to Anna or Dancer.'

'No. We don't want to alarm them at this stage. Not till we've talked to Bambini. We've no evidence that either of them is involved.'

Illya asked: 'Is there anything that we can do to help?'

'Not a thing,' Jevons said. 'I would suggest that you go back to the Savoy and catch some sleep. I'll call you as soon as there is anything to report.'

They turned out of the big gates and walked slowly back along the Embankment towards Charing Cross Underground Station. The illuminated sign above the entrance showed that the trains were still running.

A cab came cruising from the direction of Hungerford Bridge and Solo hailed it.

Illya protested: 'We don't need a taxi. We're only a few steps from the hotel.'

'We're not going to the hotel,' Solo said. 'We've got a lead the police don't know about. I've got a hunch that our little chum Merle knows more about Bambini than she's told us. Let's go.'

The door of the house in Berwick Street was standing ajar. They pushed it open and went up the stairs to the first floor. A 25-watt lamp burned on the landing in front of Merle's door. Solo pressed the bellpush and a shrill yapping came from inside the flat.

'That sounds like Blodwen's poodle,' Illya said. 'What is she doing here?'

'Probably had the same idea as we did,' Solo replied. He pressed the bell again. The yapping redoubled, but the door remained closed.

'What's going on in there?' Illya said. 'Why don't they answer?'

'I don't know,' said Solo. 'But I'm going to find out.'

He took a strip of celluloid from his pocket, eased it into the jamb of the door and ran it down towards the Yale lock. He pushed and the door opened. The little dog, yapping hysterically, burst out on to the landing. Illya managed to catch her before she bolted down the stairs.

Solo called: 'Blodwen! Merle!'

The sound echoed through the flat.

They went into the living-room. A pink-shaded standard lamp bathed the room in an intimate glow. There was no sign of Blodwen, but Merle was sitting in an armchair facing the door. Her lips were drawn back from her teeth in the caricature of a smile. Her eyes stared at them stonily. A knife was buried to the hilt in her half-naked left breast. She was very, very dead.

# CHAPTER THIRTEEN

AFTER SOLO and Illya had left the restaurant with the inspector, Blodwen ordered drinks for Solly and herself. They sat talking for a quarter of an hour, then Solly shook hands and departed. Blodwen paid the bill and went back to the hotel.

She bathed leisurely, luxuriating in the caress of the hot, scented water against her skin, and took more time than she needed over fixing her hair and face. Then she slipped off her flowered bathrobe and climbed gratefully between the sheets. This, she had determined, was going to be one night of complete relaxation. She felt she had earned it.

She was already more than half asleep when the bedside telephone rang. She picked up the receiver irritably and gave the extension number.

'A woman's voice asked: 'Yvonne?'

'Who – Merle! How the devil did you find me?'

'Never mind that.' The voice sounded strained. 'I got to see you urgent. I got some information. Can you come round?'

'I'm in bed,' Blodwen said.

'Well, bloody well get out of bed. This won't wait, I tell you. Yvonne, I *got* to see you – about you-know-who.'

'All right,' Blodwen sighed. 'Give me ten minutes to get some clothes on. Are you at the flat?'

'Yes. And, Yvonne – don't bring nobody with you. Not even your boy-friend. If you do, I won't talk.'

'All right. I'll get a taxi.'

Blodwen dressed hurriedly. As she pulled on her stockings she tried to figure out how Merle had discovered that she was at the Savoy. She had been fairly confident that she was not being followed when she left Berwick Street for the Bond Street salon where the dye had been removed from her hair.

Before she left the apartment she opened a suitcase, took out a 7.63mm. Mauser pistol in a skeleton holster and strapped it to the inside of her left thigh. There had been a note of near-panic in Merle's voice towards the end of their short conversation. There was no sense in taking chances.

She decided to leave Dolly in her basket, but as soon as she put her hand on the doorknob the little poodle came highstepping to her side. She had no intention of being left behind. Resignedly, Blodwen picked her up.

There is seldom a shortage of taxis at the entrance to the Savoy Hotel. Blodwen got one right away and it deposited her in Berwick Street within seven minutes.

She found the key of the street door in her handbag and hurried up the stairs. The door of Merle's flat was half open. She knocked, and Merle called: 'In here.'

Blodwen went through the short hall to the living-room, stopped just too late.

She saw Merle, her black eyes terrified, being held down by a swarthy young man who looked as if he were enjoying his job. Then a pad was pressed over her face from behind, and she lost consciousness.

When she came round she was lying on the stone floor of a room that had the dank smell of a cellar. The pain in her head and shoulder told her that she had been thrown there. She screwed up her eyes against the light from an unshaded bulb near the ceiling and moved her limbs experimentally. Her hands and feet were unbound. And, miraculously, she could still feel the weight of the Mauser against her thigh.

She forced herself to sit up, fighting the wave of nausea that was the aftermath of the drugged pad. She rested for a minute, then got to her feet and leaned against the wall to take stock of her surroundings.

The cellar was long and low, with steel girders supporting the ceiling. The bulb lit only the section nearest the locked iron door. The rest was in semi-darkness, but she could make out the bulk of stacked cases in the shadows.

With sudden shock she realized that the little poodle was not with her. In her weakened state the sense of loss almost unnerved her. She hoped that they had killed it painlessly and not left it to run the streets in panic. For the first time in years she cried.

But even while the tears came, her mind was working on the problem of escape. There was no hope of getting through the door. It fitted flush with the wall and there was no keyhole in its blank inner face. Yet the air in the cellar was fresh. Somewhere there must be a ventilator, perhaps even a loading shaft from the street. She moved towards the back of the cellar, her eyes searching the walls and ceiling.

She reached the first of the stacked cases, and something about their size and shape caught her attention. She looked at them more closely. They were identical with the banded cases she had seen with Illya in the farmhouse at Cwm Carrog. The cellar was one of the stockpiles for the currency operation.

Sounds outside the door brought her swiftly back under the light. She lay down as nearly as she could remember to her original position and closed her eyes.

There came a creak of hinges and then footsteps. A shoe caught her none too gently in the ribs and a man's voice said: 'Snap out of it.'

She moaned artistically and made a business of turning over. The shoe hit her again, harder this time, and the voice snarled: 'Come on, I 'aven't got all night.'

She opened her eyes. The dark-faced hoodlum she had seen in Berwick Street was staring down at her. He had a

Browning automatic in his right hand and his finger was on the trigger.

He motioned with the barrel towards the open door. 'On your feet and start walking. And don't try nothing.'

Blodwen said: 'What do you think I'm going to do? Bite you?'

'Ah! belt up.'

He stayed so close behind her that she could feel his breath on her neck as she climbed a steep flight of twenty stone stairs. He was pretty much of an amateur, Blodwen thought. A more experienced villain would have known better. It is comparatively easy to disarm a captor who fails to keep his distance.

There was an unlocked pass-door at the head of the steps. They went through it into a carpeted passage. Blodwen could smell cooking and hear the muffled sound of a dance band combo. The man prodded her with the gun barrel and said: 'Keep going.'

They came to a door on the left-hand side of the passage. The man reached past her, turned the handle with his left hand, and said: 'Inside.' He accompanied the order with a shove that sent her headlong into the room. She recovered her balance just in time to avoid crashing into a fragile table.

Anna Soo Lee watched her unceremonious entrance from her throne-like chair. She said calmly: 'I must apologize for Luigi's manners. I assure you that I did not order you to be ill-treated. I wished merely to talk to you.'

'You could have rung me,' Blodwen said. 'It would have saved us both a lot of trouble.'

Anna smiled. 'I doubt whether you would have answered my questions over the telephone.'

'Well, before we go any further, I've got a question for you,' said Blodwen. 'Where's my poodle?'

The delicate eyebrows arched. 'Poodle? I am afraid I do not understand you.'

'You understand, all right. I was carrying a poodle

when I went into Merle's flat – just before your thugs jumped me – and I haven't got her now. What have they done with her?'

'I know nothing about this,' Anna said. 'No doubt she is still in the flat... with your friend.' She smiled again. 'If you are reasonable, we shall endeavour to reunite you.'

'What do you expect to get out of me?'

'Simply a little information. You must realize I know a great deal about you already. I know, for example, that you and your friends Mr Solo and Mr Kuryakin are agents of U.N.C.L.E. I am aware that you made great nuisances of yourselves in Wales and, indeed, quite seriously hampered certain operations of the organization which I have the honour to represent –'

'Thrush,' Blodwen interjected.

'Exactly. You will notice that I used the word "hampered", not "defeated". Our plans are too carefully devised and too far advanced to be defeated by your clumsy intervention. You have been watched ever since your masquerade brought you to my club. Your quarrel with the woman called French Louise was a bad mistake. That brought you into the open.'

'Then what's your problem?'

She made a deprecating gesture. 'Please do not attempt to be facetious. I wish you to tell me exactly and in detail how far your investigations have gone.'

'That,' said Blodwen, 'will be the day.'

Anna was unmoved. She said: 'I can assure you the day has come. The only question is whether you tell me of your own free will the things I wish to know. If you do not, the alternative will be unpleasant but inevitable.'

Blodwen laughed. She said: 'I don't suppose another murder would worry you. But I won't be much good to you dead.'

'I did not mention murder. It is conceivable, however, that death might seem preferable to continued existence.' Anna rose and went to the bellpush in the wall. When she returned to her chair she said: 'No doubt you have been told many times that you are a very pretty girl.'

'So?'

'You will see.'

There was a tap on the door and Luigi entered.

Anna said: 'Bring Emile to me.'

He looked at Blodwen and grinned unpleasantly. 'Right away.' he said.

The creature with whom he returned was barely human. He was not more than five feet tall but his chest under a ragged plaid shirt measured all of forty-four inches. Long arms, gorilla-like, swung loosely as he shambled into the room. Coarse, matted black hair hung low over the vacant eyes of a cretin. The thick-lipped mouth hung half-open, showing yellow, broken teeth.

Luigi said: 'Stay!' as one would to a dog, and he halted obediently, his unfocused eyes shifting from one woman to the other.

Anna spoke gently. 'Emile,' she said, 'do you like this pretty lady?'

He turned his head slowly towards Blodwen and made an inarticulate sound halfway between a growl and a moan. She stepped back involuntarily as he reached out a paw to touch her.

Anna said: 'That is enough. Take him away.'

Then, to Blodwen: 'In a few moments Luigi will take you back to the cellar. I will give you exactly one hour in which to consider your position. If at the end of that time you have not become more amenable, I shall send Emile to persuade you. To make the experience more interesting, I have instructed Luigi to remove the light bulb. You will be able to have a pleasant game of hide-and-seek, though I fear the end will be never in doubt.'

Luigi came back and stood waiting in the doorway.

'There is still time,' Anna said. 'Are you sure you have nothing to say to me?'

'As a matter of fact, I have,' Blodwen said.

'Fry in hell, you Chinese cow.'

# CHAPTER FOURTEEN

DETECTIVE-INSPECTOR JEVONS arrived at the Berwick Street flat within minutes of Solo's telephone call. He brought his detective-sergeant with him. Hard on their heels came the police photographer, the fingerprint experts and the divisional surgeon.

'I'll want statements from you both,' Jevons told Solo and Illya. 'It's a pity you weren't candid with me in the first place. Have you touched anything?'

'Only the telephone receiver and the outside of the door,' Solo said.

'Good. There'll be enough fingerprints to check, without your dabs complicating the issue. She wasn't exactly a nun.'

He turned to the doctor, who had just finished his examination of the body. 'What's the verdict, Doc?'

'In non-technical terms, a clean stab straight to the heart, delivered from above by a right-handed assailant.'

'Man or woman?'

The doctor took off his glasses and polished the lenses. 'It would have taken a pretty hefty woman to deliver a blow of such force,' he said. 'And it was a strictly professional job. I think I should be inclined to plump for a male.'

'Time of death?'

'Give or take a few minutes, not more than an hour ago. You'll get my report in due course, but it looks a straightforward case.' He nodded, picked up his bag and hurried out of the flat.

Illya, still carrying the poodle, looked gloomily at the photographer busy with his pictures. He asked: 'What do you make of it, Inspector? Another Bambini job?'

'It could be. He knew the woman,' Jevons said. 'But it doesn't look like his style. He'd have been more likely to cut her face to ribbons. And the weapon doesn't tell us much. It's an ordinary Commando dagger. There must be thousands of them in circulation. There are no dabs on the hilt. The killer must have worn gloves. Like the doctor said, he was a professional.'

'And a kidnapper,' Solo said. 'Whoever he is, he's got Blodwen. She would never have walked out of here without the dog. It was like a kid to her.'

Jevons brought a pouch out of his pocket and began to fill his pipe. 'What was she doing here?' he asked. 'Did you know she was coming to see the woman?'

'You know as much as we do,' Illya said. 'You heard her say in the restaurant that she was going back to the hotel. We haven't seen her since.'

Jevons called to the fingerprint men: 'Have you finished with the telephone?'

'All clear, sir.'

'Good.' He picked up the receiver and dialled the number of the Savoy.

'Well, that's that,' he said at last, replacing the instrument. 'She went back to the hotel but left again with the dog shortly after eleven o'clock. She got into a taxi and the doorman heard her tell the driver to take her to this address. We'll put out a call for the cabbie, of course, but I don't suppose he'll be able to tell us much.'

The telephone bell rang. He picked up the receiver again and listened. Then his expression lightened. He said: 'Right! We'll be over.'

He turned to Solo. 'They picked up Bambini in Stephen Street. They've just brought him in. You'd better come back with me.'

The three men went down the stairs and pushed through the crowd of rubbernecks gathered around the front of the building. Reporters struggled to get at the inspector before he could gain the sanctuary of the police car.

'No statement,' he told them. 'Ring the Press room.' The car moved off, leaving them still shouting questions.

Back in his office Jevons told Solo and Illya: 'You realize that you're here quite unofficially. I can't allow you to be present while I interview Bambini. What happens after he's been charged is something else again. Maybe your people will get in touch with the Home Office and regularize the position. Meanwhile, I'm hoping you may be able to help by filling in on the background of any statement I get out of him.'

'Where is he?' Solo asked.

'Down below, in an interview room, I'm going to talk to him now. It may be a long job, so make yourselves at home.'

He picked up a buff file from his desk and went out.

After a while a constable appeared with the inevitably mugs of tea. He looked at the poodle, which was padding moodily about the room, bent down and scratched its ear. 'Nice little chap, isn't he?' he said. 'Though personally I prefer something with more meat on.'

Illya said: 'The he's a she. Is there anywhere she could get a meal and bed down for a couple of hours.'

'I think we can manage that, sir. What's her name?'

'Dolly.'

'Ah! Dolly. All right, then, Dolly girl. Let's see if we can find you a few biscuits and a drop of milk.'

When the door had closed behind him Illya said to Solo: 'Napoleon, my friend, we are wasting too much time. As the inspector said, breaking down Bambini may not be easy. I don't propose to wait.'

'There's no need for both of us to stay around,' Solo agreed. 'I'll make your excuses to the Law. You've got your transmitter?'

'That,' said Illya, offended, 'is almost an indelicate question.'

He flagged down a late-cruising cab in Bridge Street and rode to Leicester Square Underground station. The length of Newport Street was deserted and the sign over the Gloriana was dark. The double doors of the club were shut and locked.

He walked on, noting the dark form of a man standing motionless in a doorway across the street. Jevons was plainly taking no chances, even though Bambini had been arrested.

It was equally obvious that if Blodwen were in the club she could not have been taken in through the front doors. And it was a safe bet that the stake-out included coverage of the service entrance. There must be still a third way into the place.

Illya turned right into St Martin's Lane and walked in the direction of the Coliseum theatre. He saw a block of service flats in a small court. Light shone from the vestibule but no porter appeared to be on duty.

There was an iron fire escape against the far side of the building. Illya climbed it to the top floor, then stood on the guard rail and hauled himself on to the flat roof. Crouching low to avoid showing a silhouette against the night sky, he moved across the roof to the side nearest Newport Street. He made out, in the glow of the street lights, the chimneys of the building that housed the Gloriana. To get to them would mean a suicidal journey over rooftops of varying heights and slopes and dubious holding power. Illya offered a silent prayer and lowered himself over the parapet.

The climb took him fifteen minutes of sweat and fear. When he finally lay panting against the grey slates his fingers were bleeding and his ribs bruised and sore. He rested until his heart had ceased to pound, then infinitely carefully began to work his way towards a skylight.

He tried the frame gingerly. It gave under his fingers. Slowly he inched it open and shone his pencil torch into the black cavity. The light showed an empty attic. He balled his handkerchief and propped the frame half-open while he took off his shoes and hung them round his neck by the joined laces. Then he eased the sky-light open and dropped silently into the room.

The landing outside was in darkness. He flashed the torch again and saw stairs a few feet ahead. He listened a moment, then began the descent.

There were three doors opening off the landing below. He tried them, but the rooms were bare and tenantless. He went down a second flight of stairs to the first floor.

Illya breathed a sigh of thankfulness when the torch showed that the landing was covered with heavy drab matting. He sat on the stairs and replaced his shoes before going on.

Like the one above, the landing had three doors. A thread of yellow light showed under the middle of the three. Illya listened. No sound came from the room. He flattened himself against the wall, took a penny from his trouser pocket and dropped it. It made a plunking noise as it hit the matting and rolled away.

The door swung open and Dancer stepped out into the corridor. Illya's right hand, fingers stiff, chopped down expertly. As Dancer slumped Illya caught him and dragged him back to the room. He lowered him to the floor, and shut the door.

The room was evidently Dancer's living quarters. It held a divan bed with a green folkweave coverlet, two arm-chairs, a radiogram and a bookcase that contained old magazines. A bottle of John Haig, a soda-water syphon and a half-filled tumbler stood on a table by one of the chairs.

Illya took off Dancer's belt, rolled him on to his face and strapped his hands behind his back. He pulled him across the floor, propped him in the chair by the table, took the syphon and squirted soda water over his head.

Dancer groaned. His eyes opened. He looked at Illya dazedly and struggled to free his hands.

Illya said: 'If you try to shout I'll kill you. What have you done with the girl?'

'I don't know what the hell you're talking about. What girl?'

Illya took the P38 from its shoulder holster and cocked it. He said: 'My friend, I am in no mood for games. In one second I am going to shoot you right in the belly. It will take you about five hours to die and every minute will be agony. Now talk!'

The P38 came into line.

# CHAPTER FIFTEEN

LUIGI WAS A gutter rat singularly lacking in the traditional Italian courtesy. As he prodded Blodwen back to the cellar at gun-point he described with relish and in infinite detail what she could expect at the hands of Emile. It was with genuine relief that she heard the iron door clang behind him.

The darkness in the cellar was absolute. It was like being already dead, Blodwen thought. She took the Mauser from the skeleton holster strapped to the inside of her thigh, slipped out the magazine and assured herself that the shells were still there. Anna had a peculiar sense of humour. She might have found the gun, unloaded it and replaced it.

Blodwen slid the seven rounds back, rammed the magazine home and worked the jacket to slide the first shell into the chamber. With the gun in her hand she searched methodically along the wall to the rear of the cellar. Somewhere there had to be a ventilator and a possible, however remote, route to safety.

Her left hand found the first of the packing cases. She tucked the Mauser into the waistband of her skirt and began the job of levelling the stacks.

The cases were heavy, and working in complete blackness made the task even more difficult and dangerous. A slip could mean a broken leg or arm.

But the chance of escape was there. She was banking on the hope that if a ventilator existed the touch of cold air on her face would guide her to it.

The silence was broken by a sudden crackling sound like static. Then Anna's voice, distorted by an amplifier, said: 'You have five minutes left. Are you tired of being obstinate?'

Blodwen went cold. She hadn't realized how the time was slipping away.

Anna's voice came again: 'Can you hear me?'

'Yes.'

'You have now four and a half minutes. I am waiting for your answer.'

'It's still the same,' Blodwen said. 'Go jump in your murky Chinese lake.'

Though she knew the effort was wasted, she resumed her tugging at the crates. At least, she thought, their disorder would complicate the game of hide-and-seek Anna had threatened.

The crackling started again. Almost immediately Anna said: 'Ten seconds. This is the last time I shall speak to you.'

'Nothing doing,' Blodwen replied.

'You are a fool.'

There was a click as the microphone went dead.

Blodwen gripped the Mauser and waited, straining her eyes in the blackness.

Metal grated on metal. A line of grey broadened, slowly became an oblong as the door swung open. Blodwen raised the pistol. Emile's black shambling figure was framed in the dim light. She fired.

Emile made an animal howl of pain, but he came on.

She pressed the trigger again. The Mauser jammed.

The door clanged home, leaving her imprisoned with the wounded cretin. She could hear him moaning and floundering in the blackness towards her. She backed away, jerking frantically at the gun's jacket to free the mechanism.

She stumbled against a crate and almost fell. Pain seared her ankle. She bit her lip to prevent herself crying out.

Emile sensed her position. His great hand brushed her shoulder and she side-stepped barely in time to evade his grasp. She tried to run, but her injured foot gave under her and she sprawled full-length.

Emile howled triumphantly and thudded on to his knees beside her, his hands clawing at her body. She beat at him vainly with the useless gun and could feel the strength leaving her arms. She no longer expected to escape. She was trying only to infuriate him to the point of killing her outright.

Then, suddenly, inexplicably, it was over. The cretin's hands went limp and he fell forward across her shoulders. The rancid smell of his skin filled her mouth and nostrils. She could feel bile rising in her throat.

A pencil beam shone into her eyes, making her close them and turn her head away. She heard Illya's voice say: 'Hold on. You can faint when we are safely out of here.'

She lay limp while he pulled the weight of the creature from her. 'Did you kill him?' she asked at last.

'No. His skull is thick.'

'I'm glad. The poor devil isn't responsible.'

Illya raised her gently. 'You must try to get on your feet,' he said. 'We are not out yet.'

'I'll make it,' she promised. 'Give me a minute to get my bearings. What's happened to Anna?'

'I don't know. I've seen only the floor manager. He told me where to find you. After a little persuasion, of course.'

She stood up and tested her damaged ankle. The pain was bearable. She said: 'I'm ready when you are, but I wish I had a gun that worked. Have you seen anything of a character called Luigi?'

'No. Only the floor manager.'

'Well, watch out for him. He has a mean disposition.'

They went out of the cellar. Illya shut the door and pushed the bolt home. 'That should keep our friend safe,' he said.

He led the way up the steps and through the passdoor.

The corridor was empty. Blodwen whispered: 'Anna's office is along on the left.'

'We won't disturb her,' Illya said. 'We're going out through the kitchens.' He pressed her arm. 'This way.'

He held open a swing-door set in the wall at right angles to the one through which they had come. He followed her through and let it close softly behind them. He switched on the torch and the beam danced over well-scrubbed tables and gleaming white kitchen gear. Illya said: 'Straight ahead.'

Blodwen had her hand on the latch of the street door when the lights went on and a slug thudded into the wood beside her.

As she whirled and dropped to the floor, taking inadequate cover behind a bread bin, another shot sang past.

Illya, unlimbering the P38 behind a storage cabinet, asked: 'Who is the marksman with the silencer?'

'That's Luigi,' she said. 'I told you he was no gentleman.'

# CHAPTER SIXTEEN

SOLO HAD BEEN waiting for more than an hour when the inspector returned to his office. He was smiling broadly.

He said: 'We've got him. And Anna Soo Lee, too. He's coughed the lot.'

Solo said: 'Congratulations. Was it rugged?'

'Oh, he was tough at first. You never saw a better performance. But when I showed him the medallion and the Commando dagger, and told him he was being saddled with the hit-and-run and two murders, he wilted. Incidentally, he denies all knowledge of the Berwick Street job and I'm inclined to believe him. But the rest was enough. He knew we had him to rights and decided he wasn't going to carry the can alone. He made a full statement.'

'He admits killing Price Hughes?'

'Yes, but his story is that he was acting under orders. Orders from Anna Soo Lee.

'He says the old man and Anna were mixed up in some kind of big deal – he doesn't know what – and Hughes suddenly got scared and wanted to get out. Anna paid Bambini to get rid of him.'

'Where was he killed?' Solo asked. 'It couldn't have been in his own flat. The place looked as if it hadn't been lived in for months.'

'They used a girl to lure him to one of the upper rooms in the Gloriana. After the murder they kept the body in the refrigeration room behind the kitchens. Told the staff some cock-and-bull story about the wiring being out of order. Then, at the right moment, Bambini smuggled him out to the car and dumped him on Hampstead Heath.'

He put on his hat and overcoat. 'We're ready to move in on Anna. The car's waiting downstairs. Do you want to see the end of it?'

Solo said: 'I'll be right with you.'

He brought out the little black transmitter and tuned the dials. 'Illya?'

The Russian's voice came back faintly: 'What kept you? I thought you would never answer.'

'Where are you?'

'In the Gloriana. I have Blodwen with me.'

Solo said quickly: 'She's O.K.?'

'At the moment, yes,' Illya said. 'But you'd better get here fast. Blodwen has mislaid her gun, and I have only three full clips left.'

'We're on our way.'

Solo told the inspector: 'That's a real S.O.S. Illya doesn't like calling for help. He's in rough trouble.'

'He'll soon be out of it,' Jevons said. 'The Flying Squad will have got to Newport Street by now.'

Dawn was already bright in the sky when they reached the Gloriana. A policeman with the build of a heavyweight opened the car door and leaned in. He said: 'We've got a harder nut here than we expected. The club doors are solid steel, painted to look like wood. It looks as if we'll have to cut our way in with oxyacetylene. That'll take a little time and there's some shooting going on inside.'

Jevons said: 'Can't you get up to the windows?'

'We've tried it. They've got steel shutters. The place is a fortress.'

Solo asked: 'Would it upset protocol if an outsider tried something? There are two of our people in there, remember.'

The big policeman said sceptically: 'Any suggestions welcome, chum. But I don't know what you think you're going to achieve.'

Solo got out of the car and crossed the street. He took from his hip pocket what looked like a cigarette case and lighter combined. He laid the case against the doors of the club and called: 'Duck!' Then he depressed the thumb lever and threw himself flat, covering his head with his arms.

The case exploded like a grenade. In the narrow street the crash was deafening. Chips of brick and paving flew like shrapnel, spattering noisily on the roofs and sides of the police cars. When the smoke cleared the big doors were sagging inward.

'My Gawd!' the Flying Squad sergeant said. 'What was it? A pocket atom bomb?'

He led the charge into the club, with Solo close behind. They pounded together across the dance floor.

A man came running from the back quarters, clutching a sub-machine gun. Before he could steady it at his hip, a devastating right swing from the policeman flattened him.

Three shots sounded in rapid succession, followed by a fourth. Solo said: 'That's Illya. It's his call-signal.'

A Maltese with a knife foolishly tried to bar their way to the kitchen. The police sergeant picked him up bodily and threw him against the wall. His head hit the bricks with a sound like a ping-pong bat hitting the ball. He went down without a murmur.

Luigi came through the swing door with his hands held high. He knew when to turn it in. Squad men collected him with the others.

Solo went on into the kitchen. Illya and Blodwen were dusting themselves off. Illya said: 'You timed it beautifully. Those were my last four shells.'

'You're welcome,' Solo grinned.

They walked along the corridor and met the inspector coming from the dance floor. He said: 'We've cleared out the small fry. Now for the big catch.'

They found Anna Soo Lee sitting in her throne chair. Her hair was elaborately arranged and her make-up had been applied with meticulous care. She was wearing a tunic and trousers of rich white silk – the traditional colour of Chinese mourning, Solo remembered – and there were white satin slippers on her small feet. Her golden hands gripped the arms of the chair, but her face was expressionless.

She said: 'Do not stand on ceremony, please. I have been waiting for you. There are things which I must say before I go.'

The inspector began: 'Anna Soo Lee, it is my –'

She stopped him with a gesture which would have seemed appropriate in a Ming empress.

'Do not embarrass us both,' she said coldly. 'I know your stupid formula. It means less than nothing to me now. And it is to these other gentlemen that I wish to speak.

'Mr Solo, Mr Kuryakin, you have beaten me. The mission with which I was entrusted has failed. But remember, before pride betrays you, that it was but one operation among many. Thrush is invincible. Thrush will destroy U.N.C.L.E. as you have destroyed me – and as I shall now destroy us all...'

Her black eyes gleamed. Illya had been watching her hands. He saw the fingers tighten on the carved heads that decorated the uprights of the chair.

He yelled: 'Get out!' and thrust Blodwen towards the open door.

Long jets of liquid fire streamed from the gaping mouths of the carved figures. Before the men could reach the safety of the corridor in Blodwen's wake, the room was a mass of flame.

Illya said: 'I'm going back. We can't leave her.'

'Don't be a fool,' the inspector snapped. 'You'll never make it.'

'I can try.' He plunged forward, breaking free of their grasp, but couldn't cross the threshold. The heat was like a blast furnace.

Through eyes half-blinded with smoke he made out a tiny figure sitting immobile in her glowing throne.

They pulled him away. The fire was spreading rapidly. There was nothing to do but get out while there was time.

As they reached the sagging double doors and stumbled into Newport Street, the first fire bells were clanging the arrival of the pumps from Leicester Square.

They stood by the police cars and watched the smoke billowing from the building.

Illya said quietly: 'She dreamed of ruling the world. She died, at least, like a queen.'

# The Man From U.N.C.L.E.

# THE COPENHAGEN AFFAIR

by

# John Oram

Christmas in Copenhagen. A beautiful girl with a deadly secret. A package that someone would kill for ...

Napoleon Solo must defy the deadly dangers set for him by an organisation bent on his destruction – THRUSH.

# B⬛XTREE

# The Man From U.N.C.L.E.
by
Michael Avallone

In Utangaville, Africa, it took two days. In Spayerwood, Scotland, it happened overnight. In a small German town, it worked immediately.

In each place, people suddenly turned into mindless, babbling creatures who thrashed about wildly, uttering weird, half-human cries – and then died a hideous death. Doctors and scientists were baffled as to the cause. Was it a sudden epidemic, an unknown virus?

Or had THRUSH discovered a deadly new weapon for world conquest?

# The Man From U.N.C.L.E.
## THE DOOMSDAY AFFAIR
by
Michael Avallone

His name was Tixe Ylno ...

The U.N.C.L.E. files could tell nothing about him except for that code name. He could be anyone – a cab driver, a corporation executive, a scientist, a storekeeper ... ANYONE! And he might be anywhere in the United States.

But whoever or wherever he was, U.N.C.L.E. had to find him – because he controlled a secret that had the world at his mercy!

# B⬛XTREE

# OTHER PAPERBACK TITLES AVAILABLE FROM BOXTREE

### NOVELS

| | | |
|---|---|---|
| ☐ 1-85283-877-9 | The Man From U.N.C.L.E. | £3.99 |
| ☐ 1-85283-882-5 | The Man From U.N.C.L.E. The Doomsday Affair | £3.99 |
| ☐ 1-85283-887-6 | The Copenhagen Affair | £3.99 |
| ☐ 1-85283-857-4 | The Stone-Cold Dead In the Market Affair | £3.99 |
| ☐ 1-85283-791-8 | The Prisoner: I Am Not A Number! | £3.99 |
| ☐ 1-85283-830-2 | The Prisoner: Who Is No. 2? | £3.99 |

### REFERENCE

| | | |
|---|---|---|
| ☐ 1-85283-260-6 | The Prisoner and Dangerman | £14.95 |
| ☐ 1-85283-244-4 | The Complete Avengers | £12.99 |
| ☐ 1-85283-141-3 | The Incredible World of 007 | £15.99 |
| ☐ 1-85283-164-2 | Thunderbirds Are Go! | £9.99 |
| ☐ 1-85283-191-X | Stingray | £9.99 |
| ☐ 1-85283-340-8 | Star Trek: The Next Generation Technical Manual | £11.99 |
| ☐ 1-85283-277-0 | The Encyclopedia of TV Science Fiction | £19.99 |
| ☐ 1-85283-129-4 | The Boxtree Encyclopedia of TV Detectives | £17.99 |
| ☐ 1-85283-163-4 | The Boxtree A–Z of TV Stars | £11.99 |

*All these books are available at your local bookshop or newsagent, or can be ordered direct from the publisher. Just tick the titles you want and fill in the form below.*

Prices and availability subject to change without notice.

---

Boxtree Cash Sales, P.O. Box 11, Falmouth, Cornwall TR10 9EN.

Please send cheque or postal order for the value of the book, and add the following for postage and packing:

**U.K. including B.F.P.O.** – £1.00 for one book, plus 50p for the second book, and 30p for each additional book ordered up to a £3.00 maximum.

**Overseas including Eire** – £2.00 for the first book, plus £1.00 for the second book, and 50p for each additional book ordered.

OR please debit this amount from my Access/Visa Card (delete as appropriate).

Card Number

Amount £ ................................................................................

Expiry Date ................................................................................

Signed ................................................................................

Name ................................................................................

Address ................................................................................